The Genesis Seed

© Lucia Fudge 2014

Per Maria

This is a work of fiction. Names, characters, places and incidents are products of the author's imagination. Any resemblance to actual events or locales or persons, living or dead is entirely coincidental.

Chapter 1

It was a sulky, industrial landscape and Theresa hated it. She stared out the window, homesick. Her mother stood behind her and looked out, her reading glasses perched on her nose. Raucous seagulls cawed past, hunting philanthropists bearing hot chips.

"My first water view," Grace grinned at Theresa, "and it's butt ugly."

They looked across the road at the dock. From their second storey window, they looked down on its roof, splattered with seagull droppings. Oily water lapped at the wharf's pinions. Beyond the wharf, a sterile expanse of warehouses and container ships.

"I'm too old to drive twelve hours straight," Grace stretched her arms, "my shoulders are stuffed. The next time we do this Melbourne to Sydney drive, you'll have your licence, it won't be so bad then."

She shook her dark hair free from its clip and started. "Tess, we're nearly the same height. When did that happen?"

Theresa scowled at her. "You're always too busy to notice stuff. See the angels?"

"What angels?"

"See, you don't notice anything. They're everywhere, look above you."

Grace gazed upwards and wrinkled her nose. Plaster angels linked hands on the centrepiece of an ornate ceiling and stared down at her. A giant rice paper lantern covered the light bulb that hung from the centerpiece. Grace glanced about the lounge room, at the cream sofa overloaded with beaded cushions and the Persian rug that covered grey, faded wood floors.

"Too seventies boho for me. I think we'll stay a couple of weeks and then look for something better. I'm sure the company will be ok with that."

Theresa caught her breath, then exhaled sharply.
"Oh really, Mum? Another major decision you make about my life and don't bother asking me?"
"Don't start again, Tess. You can be such a drama queen."
"You're a bitch, Mum. I didn't ask to get pulled outta school in my final year. Most parents walk on eggshells for their kids this year, my teacher told me. You think moving me away from everyone in Melbourne to Sydney is ok? I hope I do crap in the exams, it'll serve you right." She turned away and looked out at the harbour.

Grace held out her hand to touch Theresa's shoulder but she shook her off. "Piss off."
"Don't speak like that, there's more articulate words to use for anger."
"Stuff being articulate, it's how I feel." She turned towards her mum. "I'm calling Nick, I said I'd call when we arrived."
"Don't be long. We've got to unpack our suitcases, first term starts tomorrow. We need to find your uniform and shoes." She smiled uncertainly at Theresa. "It'll be a good year, babes. It's a great opportunity for me to work in our Sydney office and for you to go to a private school."
"Good for who? I won't see Nick for a year."

"Rubbish, I said you could fly home to see him and your dad. I gave you an option, remember, you could've stayed with your Dad."
"Some crap option, Sarah hates me and I hate her. Those long, shiny nails and clean cupboards of hers. She's as anal as you, that's why dad married her."

"Enough! You love pointing out my failings. I never do that to you." Grace stopped, then took a deep breath. "Go call Nick. I'll call your grandparents on the mobile."

Theresa stood still. "I can't."
"What now?"
"I don't know where the phone is."
They glared at each other.
"Well find it, I'm having a bath."
"Why do you have a bath every time we argue? there's water restrictions in Sydney. You'll drain the dam."
"If it means surviving your teenage years, it's worth it." Grace flexed her shoulders again as she walked down the hallway and winced.
"Hope it's really painful" Theresa thought.
She stared out the window again and watched a train cross over the Harbour Bridge, a mechanical angel transporting city pilgrims. The beggarly cry of seagulls filled her senses.

Theresa sat at the curved window seat and looked at the open plan room. It occupied half the floor space of the flat, with a combined kitchen and lounge area. The Persian rug and cushions gave an oriental warmth to the flat. She looked up at the ceiling angels, somehow they soothed her homesick heart.

She walked down the hallway and checked the two bedrooms that lead off it to the right. The rooms were furnished in Spartan style, with ceiling angels abundant. As Theresa searched for the phone, she noticed a closed door on the left hand side of the hall. She pulled at the door knob and it slid open to reveal a compact study, with a desk, laptop computer and fax machine within.
"Found it!"

"Where?" Grace called out from the bathroom.

"Over here, other side of the hallway."

Theresa turned as her mum entered the room and she noticed a piano wedged beside the door frame.

"You cow, Mum! you said no piano this year."

Grace looked out the window, a flush on her cheeks. "I know, we agreed. You don't have to continue lessons, it's just an option, ok?"

"It's not ok but I'm used to the fact that you don't listen to me. I'm calling Nick now, I need privacy." Theresa pointed to the door.

Grace grinned. "If we stay, I'm putting in a second phone line, you'd live in here otherwise."

"Better than living with you."

Theresa pointed again. "Have a bath, Mum." She closed the door swiftly on her, then ran across to the phone and dialled.

"Hello."

"Hi, it's Theresa."

"Tess, darling, how was the trip? Is your Mum ok? I know she hates driving. What's the flat like, can you see the Harbour Bridge?"

Theresa interrupted before Mrs Vasoulos drew another breath.

"Good, good, good and yes I can see the Bridge, I can see it from my window now. Can I speak to Nick?"

Mrs Vasoulos gave her crescendo climbing laugh. "You're a nut. Nick's here, he's just going out."

Theresa closed her eyes and waited. She waited for the weightless, spinning love test. It was always there, on the phone, in a park, after school. Her connection to loving him. The phone line rattled, became mute, then clear.

"You"

"Yeah, me."

"Miss you, Tess. Did your Ma behave? Any near death experiences?"

"Ten hours in a car with my Mum is a near death experience."

He gave a low laugh. "When will you fly down?"

"Not today."

Again his low laugh and Theresa closed her eyes to hear it more intimately.

"When do you start school? what's it again?"

"Tommorow. Loreto College at Kirribilli. It's full of nice, rich girls. Mum's thrilled, there's no boys."

"You don't need to see any boys this year. Make sure you don't talk to any Sydney boys, ok? they're all gay anyway."

"I've got a harbour view."

"Rich girl. Lots of yachts and sailors, huh?"

"No, a boring dock and oily water, dead fish floating belly up. Jealous?"

Low laugh again and Theresa pressed her head against the top of the desk.

"Miss you."

"Me too. I gotta go, Tess, I'm meeting the gang at the movies."

She opened her eyes, looked out the window, heart stung. Two gulls flew into view, dive-bombed to the roof of the dock, then flew away without landing.

"Who's going?"

"Everyone. I'll call you soon. Love ya."

Her stomach tightened. "How much?"

"Wing span of a Pteranodon."

"Not big enough."

They laughed together, a love murmur.

"Bye."

Theresa stared out at the late sun and blinked. She swivelled the computer chair and opened her arms out wide. "It's a year, just a year. I'll be back."

She heard the sound of bath water running and a faint scent of lavender travelled down the hallway.

Theresa looked up at the low ceiling, no space for angels in this sensible room. In a corner of the ceiling, above the desk, a latch to an attic. Theresa looked at it casually, then found it hard to look away. The trapped sensation evoked a memory of when she was a child on a tram trip in Melbourne. On the seat opposite her had sat an extraordinarily beautiful woman and Theresa stared at her throughout the journey, the gravitational pull of her beauty hard to break. She felt the same sensation now.

Theresa looked down and noticed her hands trembled with a strange energy. She climbed onto the desk and laughed to herself. "Shit, mum would crack if she saw me near the laptop."

Her hands reached up, a blind need for upward motion within her.

Chapter 2

Theresa tugged at the latch and it gave easily. She flung the hatch backwards and positioned her head and shoulders within the small space. Darkness blinded her and the smell of old wood filled her. She blew on the floor and watched dust particles float down in semi darkness. As the dust descended, a memory rose within her to catch it.

Another late afternoon sun and a small girl stood in a shed, her bare feet warm on the concrete floor. A tall man knelt down beside her and handed her some curly brown fragments. "Hey Tessie, like some chocolate?"
She licked it and made a face. "This is funny chocolate, Daddy."
"Wood chocolate," his eyes creased "for my little Pinocchio."
She threw the shavings at him. "You're silly, Daddy!"
"That's me, silly."
He pulled her onto his lap and she squeezed her face into his neck. He smelt of sweat, shampoo, wood and love. Theresa could smell love as a little girl.

Theresa shook her head to clear the memory. She heaved herself upwards and looked about. The attic was a disappointment. It was a small room, empty except for a chair near the window. The peaked ceiling resembled a plaster exclamation mark. She tapped the floorboards to gauge their strength, then walked across to the attic window.
It was sectioned into old fashioned panels and she pushed at one. It gave way and a salty breeze sauntered into the room. Theresa leaned against the window and closed her eyes. She visualized her house in inner city Brunswick, the cluttered rooms and mossy courtyard. She remembered the day her dad left.

"Don't cry, Tessie, everything's ok. You'll have two bedrooms now, two homes."
He left quietly and she missed the warm smell of his love.

Theresa opened her eyes. "It's a memory room" she thought. She sat on the chair and felt something beneath her on the seat. It was an old leather bound book, faded and spotted. She opened the cover and a memory scent arose in her mind. Old fashioned flowers. Theresa peered at the eccentric writing on the opening page. A name at the top right hand corner: Patrizia D'Agnese.
"What language is it?" she wondered.
Beautifully sketched flowers and herbs lined the pages, she recognised parsley and basil. There was a date on the first page: 1786. It sent the hair on her arms upwards. Theresa looked out the window, the horizon appeared an endless white dune to her. She shook her head but the illusion remained. She could smell salt and hear the wash of sea.
"Oh God," she whispered "What's wrong with me?"

She closed her eyes and breathed slowly. Her eyelids twitched, tormented by a white light. Theresa kept her eyes closed, head bent towards her body in foetal protection. Wind blew her hair and she felt sand between her fingers. She opened her eyes and stared.
She sat atop a sand dune, covered in sea grass. A metre in front of her, a mangrove river flowed. She stood and shielded her eyes to the midday sun. Crows flew above the dense bushland that surrounded her. An antiquated wooden boat sailed on the river.

Voices sounded nearby. A petite girl, not much younger than herself, perhaps sixteen, walked with an older man. They stopped on the sand, oblivious to her.
"Why don't you like them, Papa?"

"When did I say I disliked them? The Macarthurs are good people. I've never said less of them."

"You never say more either. I was invited to all their dances last summer and you refused."

"I didn't!"

"You said if I came back a refined lady, you'd lose your scallywag forever."

"I was teasing, Matilda."

"Your eyes weren't." She stared at the shoreline moodily.

He nudged her. "Mr Ted's busy, he does the river run every day now."

She stayed silent.

"Perhaps he's another letter from England for you."

"What do I want with a suitor? It all ends up in slavery. I might as well stay with you, even if you're mean to me."

"Wicked girl, who puts these thoughts in your mind?"

Matilda laughed and ran ahead.

He sprinted across and held her arm. "You can dance with me, until I find you a suitable boy."

"Who then? Edmond Watts, who blushes to his earlobes if I say hello to him? Or Stephen Busby, son of a convict fraudster? We could thieve the Cove together at night and sell our takings for rum. Which of them would you choose for me?"

"Neither. I'll chain you to the kitchen chimney and give you three feet of slack to cook my dinner and nothing more if you speak like that."

Matilda grinned. "Same as a marriage then."

"Impudent girl, I'll send you to England. Your aunt'll teach you manners, none of your currency cheek there."

She laughed and snuggled up to him. "You wouldn't send me away, Papa."

He bowed to her on the sand and she curtsied. He held out his arms and began to hum an old fashioned melody. Matilda's long skirt trailed behind her as they danced on the sand. The fabric made a spider web trail on the white grains.

"Tilly, you can choose who you want for a mate, you know I'd never interfere."

She giggled as he spun her around. "Slow down, Papa, I'm dizzy!"

Theresa stared at them, puzzled. "They don't acknowledge me at all."

"Stop, Papa, the Macarthur's boat coming. They think you're mad enough as it is!"

He bowed to the boat as it sailed past between the narrow mangrove banks.

A woman wearing a flowing dress nodded and raised her fan at them from the boat.

He rolled his eyes and recommenced humming.

"See, you don't like them. That was very rude, Papa."

"She didn't see me, Tilly, the wind blew her petticoat into her eyes. The virtuous lace of Empire was upon her."

"You're so sarcastic about them. The Macarthurs are well regarded here in Parramatta. It's you that people talk about. Poor Tilly, growing up with a mad widower, who talks aloud in his fields with no one to answer him. People laugh at me when I drive past in my carriage alone on a Sunday. You won't darken a church door. A native could drag me away to the bush and you'd be none the wiser."

He spoke drily. "I'd hear you, Tilly. And they're Wann-gal people, not natives, I've raised you to have respect for them. We've pushed them away, after all."

"Govenor Phillip said it was our land."

"Phillip treated them as exotic Hottentots. Exhibits for his King and country, a living specimen of stone age man to impress the naturalists in London." He sighed.

"They're so much more, Tilly. You know that. Your mother loved them." He looked away.

"Did she?"

He fell silent.

Matilda kicked at the sand with her boot as she spoke. "You never speak of her, Papa."

He remained silent.

"I wish you did. When I was little, you'd sometimes say I was like her. I was so thrilled, I couldn't breathe. But that's all you ever said. In the end, I didn't know if it was a good or bad thing. I felt I'd failed you."

"Tilly, I never meant that. It's hard to speak of her."

"Try for me. I have everyone else's words of her but yours. I used to pretend she was still alive when I was little. I'd imagine that she'd tuck me into bed at night, then you'd come in to kiss me goodnight. It helped me miss her less."

The silence lengthened.

"We should go, Papa. It's late."

"I'll try, Tilly. I promise."

They walked on and wind erased the traces of their footsteps. Theresa lay on the warm sand and closed her eyes. Gradually, the heat subsided on her skin and darkness bore down on her eyelids. She jerked her eyes open, looked at the shadowy attic that surrounded her. Her hands shook as she walked across to the window. Pale stars shone from the sky, diminished by city lights.

A palsy overtook her limbs as the calm of her illusion vanished. She wanted to move but she was afraid.

"Tess, where are you? If you're still on the phone, you're dead." Grace pushed open the study door. "I hope you're not planning to walk back to Melbourne."

"Mum."

"Tess?"

"I'm here."

Grace looked up as her daughter's voice reverberated through the ceiling.

"Where's here?"

"In the attic. Can you come up?"

"Are you ten years old? Get down please, what if you fell on my laptop? It costs a fortune."

"Shut up, Mum." Theresa dangled her legs over the attic opening, then jumped onto the desk.

"Careful! Now explain please, what possessed you?" Grace saw her daughter's ashen face. "What's wrong, babe?"

"Nothing!"

Theresa ran down the hallway to her bedroom and slammed the door. Then she did it again. On her third try, Grace's foot appeared in the doorway.

"Enough! just be grateful I don't kill you. Our new neighbours will probably wish I did after that tantrum. I'm going to bed, I suggest you do the same."

Theresa lay face down on her bed and smelt the strange linen. New shadows on the floor and sounds from her window. The hallucination shocked her and she closed her eyes to bring back safe memories. She remembered a wet Melbourne day, the end of school term last year.

Young children struggled into bright raincoats, the primary colours of childhood. Umbrellas raised, the smell of rain on concrete. Theresa had smiled at them as she walked past within a circle of friends. She had no umbrella but Nick's hand was warm and dry. They crossed the road from school and entered the park, as Nick's hand led her home.

Theresa turned over on her bed and stared at the ceiling. A plaster angel stared down at her and she thought it was smiling faintly in the dark.

Chapter 3

It felt wrong to Theresa.

Grace pointed to the street directory on her lap. "Tess, look up the exit to North Sydney, I know it's soon after we cross the Harbour Bridge. Please, babes."

As Theresa bent over the map, her blazer creaked with starch.

"It's this one coming up, stay in the left lane. Don't panic, ok?"

Grace nodded. "Ok, thanks. Now I do an immediate loop to the right, the Principal told me. It's easy from here."

"Is she nice?"

"Lovely, we'll meet at her office for a tour and then go to your classroom. I don't know how we're going to do this sprint across the Bridge every morning, it's an 8.30am start. Just another ball to juggle." Grace sighed.

Theresa smiled at the image of her mum juggling balls marked "work" "school" and "daughter". She thought about the hallucination the previous night and shuddered to herself.

Grace hit her hand on the wheel of the car and whooped.

"This is it, Kirribilli! it looks like San Francisco, all hills and indecently expensive property."

Theresa looked out as the Sydney sun blazed down. She imagined leaving their Brunswick terrace and walking along the narrow streets to her school. Nick and her friends walking together, under changeful Melbourne skies.

"Mum"

"Yes?"

"It doesn't feel right."

"Don't start, Tess, I can't hear that stuff again. You were the weirdest kid with your stomach." Grace frowned as she stopped at a street corner. "I can't see a thing, the signs are as bad as Melbourne's!"

A group of school girls walked past and she relaxed back in her seat. "Bingo, we can follow the school uniforms."

"Mum, speed up! they'll think we're stalking them." Theresa crouched in her seat, she felt like vomiting into her boater hat.

"Ok, we're here." Grace pulled over and her business smile appeared.

Theresa tried to open the car door as her stomach churned.

Grace waited on the pavement. "Let's go."

"No," she put her head on her backpack "I'm not." Her blazer creaked again.

"Tess, talk to me, not the bag."

Loreto girls filed past as Grace crouched down discreetly beside her. "It just feels weird and new, it will pass by the end of the week. This is a great opportunity, we couldn't afford to do this in Melbourne, my salary wouldn't cover the school fees. With the house rental, we can. Please, babes."

"No."

Grace's neck stiffened "What do you expect me to do?" She threw her handbag onto Theresa's lap. "How do I explain this to the Principal? You're just scared."

"It's not me. It feels wrong."

"Shit, give me a break, stop the world for my daughter. I start work today, new office, new job and I know no one. I don't feel hugely good myself."

Theresa got out of the car and shook her blazer off. "I'm goin home"

"What, to Melbourne?"

"No, the flat."

"Don't do this to me, just try one day." In the simmering heat, Grace's mind slipped back to a memory.

A child hid under an upturned car seat.

"No, Mama, I won't go, I won't!"

Grace knelt beside her. "Please, Tessie, you'll love it. Pre School's lots of fun. There's a playground and play dough and toys. Just try it."

"No."

Mothers walked past her curiously, as they held the hands of their obedient children.

A bell sounded and Grace started back to the present.

"Mum, can I have some money?"

"You're serious. Do you realise how embarrassing this will be for me?"

"I couldn't give a shit, I didn't ask to come here. Ok, I'll walk home."

Grace called out. "You don't know the way."

"I'll find it, I'm seventeen."

"Tess, please!"

"Bye, Mum."

"Wait" Grace ran to her.

"Babes, I'm sorry. We'll try again."

"No" Theresa took the note handed to her. "Thanks."

"C'mon, I'll drive you."

"No, I'll catch a bus or a train, it's only across the Harbour Bridge. I'll swim to the Rocks if I have to."

Grace's eyes glowed. "Don't joke with me, I'm not up for it."

She slumped across the car door and looked at her watch. "It's only 8.30 and I'm exhausted."

Theresa moved towards her, then stopped. She turned and walked away, her legs trembling. Past the school grounds and the pristine houses. Past it all.

Chapter 4

Grace stared out the fifteenth floor window. "Big city."

"You're not from Hicksville yourself, Melbourne's as big. Just not as interesting."

Grace grinned at Anna, her petite, new secretary. "I can see the Melbourne jokes coming. To summarize Melbourne's superiority, you don't have trams, a decent AFL team or four seasons in one year. Or one day, for that matter."

"2005 Premiership to you."

"Really? I never watch football," Grace sighed. "I can't even insult my staff properly."

"Just call some of your predecessors for pointers on that."

Anna watched her stare out the window again. "You looking for someone?"

"Yes, she's seventeen and she hates me."

"Teenager, I had two of 'em. Don't worry, she'll love you when she's about thirty, she might need a free babysitter by then."

"Mine won't be having kids. Said it was unlikely she could raise them to be normal, given her highly dysfunctional background. By the time she's off the psychiatrists' couch, her ovaries would've shrivelled up and died."

Anna's freckles and sun spots dissolved into a smile. "She's not in school?"

"Should have started year twelve today. Theresa walked out of the car and I couldn't stop her. See, I manage a Human Resources Department but I can't manage my own daughter."

The phone beeped.

"Yes, I'll tell Grace you'd like to see her. 11am in the boardroom."

Anna looked across. "Mr Gordon would like to introduce you to our other senior executives."

"Five minutes to eleven, I see he gives plenty of notice. I've only spoken to him on the phone, is he a nice bloke?"

"He's a bloke."

"Oh dear. Never mind, I'll serve up my Melbourne charm, that's something else we have down south, imbue it in our mother's milk." She stood and straightened her skirt. "If you spot a tall, scowling dark haired girl, let me know."

"Will do boss, nothing's too hard for a Sydney secretary."

"Where's the boardroom?"

"End of the corridor, last on the left. And don't worry about your girl, she'll be ok. Has she run away before?"

"Anna!"

"Just kidding"

"Sydney humour's an acquired taste."

"Enjoy it while it lasts, you won't get any in the boardroom. Y'know, my youngest went to Tafe, she couldn't handle senior school. It was best for her, she was a really unusual kid."

"Anna, are you a part time psychologist?"

"Part time miracle worker, part time saint. Always overworked and invariably underpaid. Scoot, boss, you'll be late."

"Why do my secretary's always give me advice?"

"You just have that sort of face."

Grace laughed to herself as she walked down the hallway.

....

Theresa stopped on the pedestrian walkway of the Harbour Bridge and looked down. Sydney was impossibly beautiful. Like her Mum's funky jazz music, it had the same ability to elate her. The Opera House resembled a giant collection of sea shells blown in from the Pacific, nestled in an emerald bay.

"Nick would love this!" She walked on, boater hat in hand.

She walked down the stairs to the Rocks district below the Harbour Bridge. She loved the quaint sandstone shop fronts and terraces. It felt like home, Brunswick with a classy facelift. An elegant carriageway entrance to convict history.

A fluffy cat snoozed in the sun as Theresa walked past the Victorian terraces on her street.

"I hope Mum doesn't feel like total crap." she thought as she pushed open the wrought iron fence. Seagulls splattered white waste onto the courtyard.

"Hope that's not a sign!" she grinned to herself.

As she opened the front door, voices sounded from within.

"Yes, that's perfect. Practise the piece this week."An older woman stood with a young man at the staircase.

"Same time next week, Madame Maruska?"

"Absolutely, bar death or senility. Remember, you are Mozart incarnate."

Theresa stood aside as he passed her.

The older woman approached her with a smile. "Hello, you must be Theresa. I'm Maruska, I live in the downstairs flat. I met your mother last night. How do you like Sydney?"

"It's cool," Theresa looked at her curiously. "Why'd he call you Madame Maruska?"

"My stage name. A lifetime ago, I was a concert pianist. Would you like to come in for a cup of tea? My next student doesn't arrive for half an hour."

"Sure, thanks."

She followed Maruska into a large kitchen at the back of her flat and stared at the cultured chaos around her.

The kitchen was an original 1920's design, with small cupboards and a single sink. A Kookaburra stove stood in immaculate condition, dried bay leaves, lavender and oregano hung above it in bunches. A sprinkle of cracked herbs lay on the floor. Low book shelves lined two walls, pottery and marble busts littered their tops. An eclectic collection of leather bound books filled the shelves.

Prints of early Australian artists hung on cream walls. Theresa walked over to examine a print of Sydney Cove.
"What do you think of my housekeeping?"
"I wish my Mum had your standards."
They both laughed.
"I'll try to train her."
"That's impossible, she's from an Italian background, cleaning's her only hobby. Do you ever tidy up?"
"Never, I'd be wiping away the soul of good days past."
"Cool line."
"Be my guest to use it."
Maruska poured water into a blue and white flowered tea pot. "Be a cherub and collect some cups and saucers from the cabinet behind you."
Theresa selected two from the mismatched collection.
"Show me your hands."
Theresa held them out, the odd request perfectly ordinary in this extraordinary room.
"How long have you played piano?"

"How'd you know?"
"I guessed. You haven't answered my question."
"Since I was five, I don't play now."
"Shame, music shapes your hands and your mind. I'm sure the desire will come back." Theresa sipped her tea. "How long have you lived

here, Maruska?"

"My whole life, I inherited the house from my parents."

"Wow, you must've seen a lot."

"Everything and yet very little. Human emotion's the same wherever you go."

Theresa opened her mouth to speak, then closed it.

"What were you going to say?"

"Um, did you ever go into the Attic when you were young?"

"All the time, it's the most exciting room in the house."

Theresa stared at her teacup. "Did you ever see any weird things? Things you can't explain?"

"Yes, that's the charm of an attic." Maruska's hazel eyes gleamed "Visit the attic any time you like. The view becomes more extraordinary with every visit."

She glanced up as a buzzer sounded.

"Now there's my next pupil. Off you go, cherub. Thank you for staying to tea. We'll become good friends, I can tell."

Theresa walked upstairs to her flat, guided by Maruska's hand. Her heart felt remarkably lighter.

Chapter 5

"Don't call me Ma!"

Theresa giggled. "Yes, Ma."

"Tess, stop it! I'm still annoyed about this morning, you didn't have to see the Principal and explain your no show. I put it down to nerves, by the way. You'd better look highly strung tomorrow."

Silence.

"There's chicken in the freezer," Grace continued. "Can you put it in the microwave on defrost and chop some capsicum."

"Ok." An angry click.

Grace listened to the disconnected dial tone.

Anna glanced up. "All ok, boss? the meeting went well?"

Grace's eyes came back to the present. "Absolutely, Ralph's charming."

"How come your two predecessors in the last eighteen months disagreed? I'm beginning to think it's me."

"Obviously they were free spirits. My daughter assures me that I have no life, thus I am the perfect corporate slave."

"Must be a Melbourne thing." Anna placed a pile of correspondence in front of her. "Boss, here's the first chain in your servitude."

Grace sighed as she scanned them.

Theresa. glanced at her watch, nearly 3pm. Nick and her friends would be walking home from school soon. "My last year of school, why didn't she let me finish it at home?" She felt restless. "I need to....." her thoughts trailed off.

She stared blankly at the worn timbers of the wharf outside, like a grey allegory of her life. Suddenly it clicked within her and she ran to the study. Theresa climbed the desk and pulled herself through the attic latch.

She sat on the chair and held the aged diary in her hands. "I need...." she muttered.

Thunderous stomps echoed around the room and Theresa started in fear. She looked up at the ceiling.

It vanished.

She looked at the whitewashed walls.

They vanished.

She felt the floorboards buckle beneath her and screamed as she fell into space. The descent blinded her.

Cascading water and an aroma of moss suffused her senses.

Theresa felt her forehead, shakily. At her feet, a pattern of midnight blue, white and gold mosaic tiles. She touched them and gasped. "I'm hallucinating again, it'll go away."

She looked up and began to cry. "Oh my God!"

The attic was transformed into a palatial courtyard, illuminated by grey light. Marble statues of musicians lined the rectangular walls, the folds of their antiquated dress moved with their silent musicianship. A young man played the flute as his cape swirled in time. A pretty girl played the harp as her curls brushed the strings. A lute player tapped his foot as he played.

Mossy walls enveloped the musicians in a wintery garden of Eden. Giant terracotta pots rested on the mosaic floor and in the centre of the courtyard stood a fountain. Cascading water broke the silence.

A door opened nearby and a petite young woman stepped out into the evening, an emerald shawl wrapped around her shoulders. Theresa knew it was a winter's evening yet she still felt warm. The woman cupped her hands at the fountain to drink, a cloth bag by her side. Through an open doorway at the back of the courtyard, the powerful stomps sounded again.

"Horses," Theresa breathed, "it's the sound of horses."

"Buona Sera, Signorina Patrizia."
Theresa saw an elderly man standing in the back doorway, a black cane in his hand, the handle lined with mother of pearl.
The young woman looked up from the fountain. "Buona Sera, Signore Eduardo."
"They can't see me," Theresa's heart welled with sadness. "I don't belong in their world."
She examined them closely. Patrizia wore a long black dress, with a delicate bustle at the back. Eduardo wore breeches and a flowing cape over his small frame. Their antiquated dress puzzled Theresa.

Patrizia ran across the tiled floor, lifting her skirt with one hand. Eduardo raised an eyebrow. "Don't let the Medicis see you do that. The Count disapproves of ankles being displayed in his palace."
"Except if they're his mistresses'"
The old man laughed. "You're right. And Madame Medici isn't much better."
"Really? but she's so old. She can't have taken a lover, she's at least forty."

"The perfect age to start. Married life begins to pall, the children are cantankerous and the husband even more so. She meets a young man at market or in the salons and so it begins."
Patrizia wrinkled her nose.
"You're fastidious, you want the perfect man."
"I don't want any man."
"This age of romantic literature's dangerous, women seek an ideal man."
"Not me."
"Entirely you. I see young men weeping into their velvet gloves all

over Florence as you sweep past them, formulating a remedy of dried pig trotters in your head."

She laughed. "Velvet gloves probably conceal lily white hands."
"I'd like to see you settled, Patrizia."
"Just like Mama and my aunts. Someone to impregnate me and keep me busy with a tribe of children. No time for studies then."
"I didn't say that!"
"I know you all talk behind my back."
"I've never meet your Mama, how could we conspire together? I'm a black sheep too, remember?"

She grinned and linked arms with Eduardo. "How are the ladies of Florence behaving?"
"Like demons in front of my canvas. I'm tired of flattering them."
Her eyes twinkled. "Is that all you do?"
"I don't tell secrets. All gossip stops when I put down my paintbrush."
"I see. Is Madame Fortuna over her cold?"
"What cold? she bares her chest for the canvas like a whore on her lover's bed. I don't know where the Count will hang the portrait when I'm done."
"In his mistress' chambers?"
"You're too wise for your years."
"I keep company with you."
"If my hands weren't frozen in this wind, I'd slap you."
She laughed. "Come, walk with me."

Theresa followed them, enchanted. She glanced at the statues again, the musicians seemed to bow to her in the dusk, their concert ended.
They passed through the back doorway. It led to a narrow

cobblestone street, lit by fire lamps. Carriages clattered past as the chilled snort of horses reverberated against the walls.

Theresa held her hands up to catch the falling snow flakes as she listened to their conversation.

"I miss the sun, Patrizia."

"Me too. Mama's hands are crippled with arthritis now. I still haven't found the perfect mix of herbs to treat her."

"You still concoct your witches brews?"

"They're not! I'm continuing a tradition started a millennium ago by Paracelus. "

"We all die in the end, Patrizia."

"But we don't have to poison each other along the way. The apothecary's treated like a god of science and nature's dismissed as old fashioned. Do y'know, Madame Medici had Tomaso bled this last summer? He's seven years old! I watched him wither away each week." Her eyes sparkled. "Finally, Madame agreed to a course of herbs. Last week, Tomaso sat in class with his siblings and was as lively and obnoxious as them!"

"God's blessed you with passion. We'll have to find the right man to bestow it on."

She rolled her eyes. "It always comes back to men."

"Either that or you'll be an eccentric old woman, dolling out remedies to outcasts. Past admirers will look at you with horror."

"I hope so."

He shook his head and they walked awhile in silence.

Theresa watched the snow flakes collect on the pavement as she followed them.

"Where else have you lived, Signore?"

"Other than Italy? France and Spain. I miss the everyday discoveries of light and colour in those countries. You continue your studies, I understand passion."

"Thanks." She hesitated "Did you ever....I mean did you ever come close .."

"To marriage? No. But love, yes."

"Who was she?"

Eduardo was silent.

"I'm sorry, I feel I know you like a father. I shake off my governess persona and I'm myself."

He spoke softly. "A Spanish girl of the sun. I knew her in my second year of residency at the palace in Madrid."

"Did she love you?"

"She never said so, I never asked."

"Why?"

"She was governess to the Princes' children, proud like you. I painted her once, in a portrait of the royal children. I was forbidden to paint her eyes, royal eyes were not to be immortalised with those of servants. But I caught her spirit nonetheless, her intelligent demeanour, the dark tresses of her hair and the slope of her shoulders."

"Why didn't you pursue her?"

"Because her free spirit equalled mine."

Patrizia shook her head. "I don't understand. She's the one you should've chased."

"Of course," he murmured "if I loved her less."

She stared at him, perplexed.

"She saw me as I was."

"That's good."

"Not then. I wasn't a dissolute young man but I was rebellious." He snorted. "The noble faces I painted, clothed in satin and jewels, rancid with hypocrisy. I resolved to be honest with women but never a hypocrite. If I married her, I would have been."

Eduardo smiled at the expression on her face.
"I wouldn't have been faithful. I loved the freedom my palette gave me, it took me to palaces and monasteries. I breathed the words of the wise and of fools. It gave me women that opened their hearts and bodies to me."
He looked down as he continued on. "She caught me once, unawares. I was sketching a model and Claudine came to announce that the youngest prince was ready to pose for me. She saw the look in my eyes. We never spoke of it but her eyes changed too."

Patrizia squeezed his arm.
"I left soon afterwards and moved to France."
"Did you think of her?"
"Not till many years later. I wondered if she married or left Spain to travel with the Princes' family."
"What a pity you didn't search for her."
"No, it was better to just remember."
Theresa caught her foot on a cobblestone as they turned a corner and she fell. Under a lamp, she saw blood gleam on her knee. She lifted a clump of snow and applied it as a compress. Theresa had lost sight of them as she limped on.

Ahead lay a cavernous piazza, a frozen fountain in its centre. Marble angels held hands at the base of the fountain, unearthly comrades against the snow drift.
A peddler called out. "Books for sale, philosophy, geography, botany. Books for sale!"
Patrizia and Eduardo examined the collection of books on a cart near the fountain.
Theresa approached them in relief, her breath fevered.

Patrizia shivered. "Did you feel that gust of wind?"
Theresa hung back, uneasy at her words.
Eduardo held a book up. "Does this interest you?"
Patrizia glanced at the title and started. "No, thanks."
His eyes twinkled as he spoke to the peddler. "Culpepper's Pharmacopoeia of Herbal Medicine. Seems the perfect book for a young woman who loves to fossick in summer fields. What d'you think, peddler?"

The peddler blew into his hands and pulled his scarf higher. "I'm thinking good sir, that you should purchase the book for the young lady. That way, she's happy and I'm fed."
"Done. How much?"
"Enough for a good meal and a bottle of wine."
"Here, enough for a week. You're a godsend on a frozen night."
The peddler tugged his cap and began to pack away his cart.

Eduardo handed the book to Patrizia and her face radiated as if lit by an inner lantern.
"I don't know how to repay you, Signore."
"See how good God is to me. A young woman reflects my image in her eyes and it heals me."
She squeezed his hand and they walked on. An amphitheatre of sandstone buildings surrounded them and Theresa gazed up at their elegant proportions.
They parted in a laneway. Eduardo bowed to Patrizia and then slowly walked on.
"Stop, Signore!" Patrizia ran after him.
He paused in the snow and she kissed him.
"You said once that you'd like to paint me," She said breathlessly. "I have Sunday afternoons free."
He kissed her hands and nodded. "We'll meet at my apartments at

2pm."

Theresa stood in the street as a wind spun around her.
"It's another illusion, I'll wake soon." she thought.
The wind raised to a whirlpool and she was unable to move against
its force. She tried to scream but couldn't.
Silence.
Theresa opened her eyes and stared at the attic. She threw the book
down and clambered out of the hatch. "I'm never goin' up there
again, that book's got drugs in it!"
She ran to the window seat, sat in the sunshine and put her head
against her knees. Her forehead felt moist.
She looked down and her heart stilled. Her right knee bled and on
her shorts lay a pile of melting snowflakes.
"Oh my God," she whispered, "it was real."

Chapter 6

Grace stood at the kitchen sink and whispered a prayer. Shadows ringed Theresa's eyes as she sat hunched at the table, eating toast.

"Shit," Grace thought. "I didn't know Tess would find it so hard in Sydney. I thought it'd be an adventure for us. I knew crap all, as usual."

She turned and smiled briskly. "We leave in ten minutes, babe."

"Ok"

"Is your bag packed?"

Silence.

"Tess, what's up? You look so tired, are you sleeping? Please tell me, I'm worried about you."

Theresa shrugged her shoulders.

"Babes, just say it. You were so quiet last night, you didn't even call Nick. I prefer shouting to silence, it makes me nervous."

"I'm ok, Mum." She carried her plate to the sink. "Let's go, we'll be late."

Grace felt tears collect inside her as she picked up her brief case. "You're right, let's go."

As they walked downstairs, the purple door to the first floor flat opened and a phone book was kicked against it.

"Hello," a man smiled at them from the doorway, "you're the Melbournites, my quiet, new neighbours." He resembled a sunburnt native animal, his muscular limbs tanned by life long exposure. "I'm Peter Mauldon." He extended his right hand, the fingers unexpectedly long and fine.

Grace stepped forward. "Hi, I'm Grace Ransini and this is my daughter, Theresa. Sorry we can't stop and chat, we're doing the

mad school bolt. I'm sure we'll see you again though."
"Absolutely," said in a dry tone. "I can see your daughter's thrilled to be here."
Theresa stopped on the stairs and stared at Peter blankly.
"Oh, babes, what's up?" Grace hugged her.
The purple door closed softly behind them.
"It's all wrong, Mum. I shouldn't be here, I can feel it."
"You miss everyone, I know."
"Not just that..."
"All the self help books I've read," Grace thought, "amount to nothing when I'm with her." She spoke softly. "We can't go back, Tess. I've accepted the job."
"I know."

"Where to from here? You can't sit in the flat all day, waiting for the year to pass. Nick's moving ahead, he'll be at Uni next year, you've got to keep up with your friends."
"Yeah, I know."
"Stay at home today, babes. I'll see what I can do."
"You're not gonna call Dad? I can't live there."
The purple door opened behind them again.
"No, just give me a day. It'll be ok."
Grace stood up, pressed her skirt with a nervy hand. She kissed Theresa's head and felt her shrink backwards.
"Look around the Rocks if you like, just don't get lost. I must dash, babes. I'll see you tonight."
"Thanks, Mum."
Grace walked down the stairs and opened the front door. The sun made her squint, her eyes filled and she blinked. She opened the car door and threw her case inside. "Shit, shit, shit!"
She switched on the engine and stared at the empty passenger seat beside her.

"You gonna sit on the stairs all day?"

Theresa looked up at Peter and shrugged. "Maybe."

"Could be a congestion problem."

She shifted sideways as he sat beside her. "You Melbourne girls like your space, I had a girlfriend like that once."

"What happened to her?"

"She moved back to Melbourne, couldn't stand the congestion."

She grinned and he nudged her.

"Since you've been let off the lead for the day, come out with me for a cappuccino. You can tell me all about your Mum's failings as a parent, I'll play devil's advocate. I'm told I'm a natural."

She hesitated.

"Go on, you'll be safe with me. Maruska can vouch for my good moral character."

"Ok, just let me get changed."

"Excellent idea, not good for me to be seen with a girl in a school uniform. I'd pass for a dirty old man."

Theresa smiled.

"I know what you're thinking. I was a dirty young man once but I gave it up years ago, too exhausted."

She blushed deeply.

"Go girl, I'll wait here."

The buzzer sounded and Maruska walked down the passage to let her student in. She glanced up at the stairs.

"Morning, Peter. How's the new painting progressing?"

"Bogged, coffee with a pretty girl will inspire me."

Theresa ran downstairs, slim in a tee shirt and leggings.

Maruska motioned a young woman down the hallway. "Go, I'll be in shortly."

She turned to Theresa. "Good morning, cherub. Have you visited the attic?"

Theresa whitened.

"Don't be afraid, you're meant to see it. All will unfold as it should. Enjoy your cappuccinos. Look after her, Peter."

Peter raised an eyebrow. "A very mysterious chat, what's all that about?"

"Nothing."

His languid motion reminded her of a lazy circus acrobat as they walked along the street. "We'll go to my favourite café on George Street. Coffee so strong, it makes me weep."

Theresa noticed weeds poke through cracks in the pavement as they walked the quiet streets. As they reached the café, he waved her to a table. "Morning, Isabelle. How are we this fine morning?"

An older brunette woman stood at the counter, her hands on her hips. "Is that another daughter?"

He shook his head and she waved her finger at him. "I'll be a wise monkey and ask no questions. Your usual?"

He nodded and held up two fingers.

They sat in silence as their coffees were brought over.

"How do you like Sydney?"

"It's ok, I miss my friends. And Nick, heaps."

"Boyfriend?"

"Yeah."

"It's hard being apart, isn't it? I missed my girlfriend badly when I first moved to Sydney, drove up to see her every weekend in the first year."

Theresa focussed on his hands. They were long and stained with paint streaks and she motioned to them. "Do you work from home?"

"I do, I paint."

"What do you paint?"

"Not much," She laughed as he continued on. "When I do, it's mostly landscapes. People are too hard to capture. And too unattractive."

His face twitched, the lines worn in by sun creased his smile. "Except for pretty girls."

She blushed and changed the subject.

"Did your girlfriend move to Sydney?"

Peter looked at the ochre walls of the café as he spoke.

"No. I thought we'd be together forever, she'd be my muse and I'd be a world famous artist. She saw it differently, she married a farmer two years after I left, had four kids and lived happily ever after." He lifted an eyebrow. "At least she could have realised her awful mistake and begged me to come back."

They laughed.

"And what does your elegant mum do?"

"Lots, she manages a Human Resources Department."

"Oh, a busy and important woman. Do you wanna be busy and important too, one day?"

"Um, I dunno. I haven't decided what I'll do next year."

"HSC this year?"

"Yeah."

"My kid did it last year. He's doing Arts at Sydney Uni now, till he grows up and decides what he wants to do."

"Does he live with you?"

"Nup, With my ex. All my ex's have my kids."

"How many are there?"

"Ex's or kids?"

"Both."

"Two of each."

"Whoa, spread the love, that's so seventies!" She blushed as soon as she said it.

Peter spoke dryly. "And expensive."

"Do your ex wives know each other?

"I didn't ever marry."

Theresa opened her mouth to speak, then closed it again.

"Very good Melbourne manners. It's ok, you can ask. I couldn't be tied down, they all knew that."

"Yeah, sure." Her eyebrows creased together in desperate thought for conversation. "Great coffee."

"Isn't it? and prettiest waitresses in Sydney."

Isabelle smirked as she stopped to collect their cups. "You're being professionally charming, Peter. Stop it."

"Not at all" he stood up and placed a note on the table "I've gotta head back, the gallery wants my next painting by the end of the decade. Walk back with me, Theresa?"

"No, I'm gonna look around, maybe walk to the Opera House."

"You should do a walking tour of the Rocks, if you like that kinda thing. My youngest does. I'll introduce you to Willow when she stays over next. She's a great kid."

"Ok, that'd be wicked. Thanks for the coffee."

He waved as he walked back to the docks.

Theresa turned into George Street and absorbed the new sounds of the city.

. . . .

Grace stared at the document on her desk.

"It's in English but you'd never know it, Anna. This is the most spectacularly worded staff complaint I've ever read and it's only my second day here."

"We don't muck about in Sydney. Who where you on the phone to before? I heard you mention Tafe. Is your girl digging in her heels about the new school?"

"More likely digging the nails in my coffin. I rang Ultimo Tafe, thanks to your advice yesterday."

"Always free, always bountiful."

"They accepted her, said challenging kids were always welcome." Grace suppressed a grin. "From the Registrar's tone of voice, I think she thought I was the challenging one."

"Never, boss. Theresa will like it, free spirited kids need less structure. My girl went stir at school, the bells and daggy uniforms. How's Theresa coping with the changes in her life?"

"Not so good, her boyfriend and dad's in Melbourne. Y'know what it's like at that age, Anna, all they want is to be near their friends. I'm the bitch of the universe for pulling her away, especially in HSC year. My career comes first, she thinks."

"You'd be homesick too. Nice man in Melbourne?"

"No time, Tess is high maintenance. My ex has a wife, I think another relationship on top of that would be cruel. Theresa needs to adjust to her first."

"Of course," said politely. "So what made you come?" Grace stared at her black desktop. "I was drowning, stuck in a well of sympathy and support. We're the first couple to divorce on both sides of our families. My girlfriends are great but they're settled, either married or in relationships. I was floating, I belonged nowhere, I felt nothing."

Grace watched a sea plane fly into wispy clouds from her window. "I just wanted to feel something after all those years of feeling nothing, even if it was fear or crap." She smiled. "I've had lots of crap so far."

"It'll get easier with Tess, my kids turned out ok. Y'know what your problem is? You've just got one girl and you obsess over her every upset."
Grace's eyebrows lifted as Anna continued.
"One of my girlfriends is the same, she dissects her son's every emotion. Kids are more resilient than we give them credit for. Give her space."
Anna stood and swung her handbag onto her shoulder.
"You're lucky I don't charge for these consultations, my girlfriends usually shout me dinner. I'm going to lunch, boss. Hold the office together till I get back."
She sashayed out the door as Grace laughed to herself.

Chapter 7

Discord swirled around Theresa and she loved its revolutionary rhythm. She sat at a café table and watched Tafe students walk past, maps in hand as they looked about.

A girl at the table opposite stared at her. "You new?"

"Yeah"

"What course you doin?"

"Year twelve, HSC."

"Hey, me too. Alicia." The girl smiled as she rested her head on a thin hand.

"I'm Tess. Do you know where to go for our classes?"

"You mean, other than people telling me where to go?"

Theresa pulled at her denim skirt and crossed her arms as Alicia walked across. She was a Gothic, she wore a black shirt and long skirt, tied at the waist with a black silk scarf. On both arms, jet necklaces were wrapped into bracelets and she wore an amber ring on her index finger. Black drop earrings fell from small, white ears. Black nail polish and lipstick darkened the canvas of her pale features.

Theresa grinned. "I didn't know Goth's wore ponytails."

"They don't. I tried the spiky, unwashed look but it only lasted a week. I can't do grunge and I can't stand looking dirty. Do I look a dork?"

"Nup, heaps better than me."

"I was scared I looked like a cheerleader Goth. Or Holly Golightly goes Goth. It's so tragic to look fake." Alicia smoothed a hand over her skirt. "Black feels so right now."

"Why?"

"Dunno, I just feel black. What're your subjects?"

"English, modern and ancient history, economics and maths. You?"
"Same, except no economics, I'm studying textile designs. I'm gonna be a fashion designer."
"Wicked, are you gonna use any other colour than black?"
"Nup, not for a few years. If I get really cheerful, I'll throw in some grey. C'mon, I'll walk you to D block. Sounds like prison, huh?"

Theresa followed behind her.
The journey to Tafe had been rich in visual snapshots that stirred her senses all morning. Bus drivers accelerated through amber lights on George Street. Loitering pigeons escaped death by quick wings. Pretty girls walked the pavement in pastel heels.
The chaos of imperial Chinatown as children walked hand in hand with Mama. Victorian shop fronts with long gone merchants chiselled into sandstone facades. Empty Cathedrals. Languid students in cafes. The theatrical facade of Ultimo Tafe.

Alicia was oblivious to the crowd that parted in front of her as they entered D building. Their classroom was small and windowless, a blank canvas for the mix of races within. Theresa lowered her eyes as she walked to the back of the room.
A dark haired boy motioned to Alicia's clothes and she stuck her tongue at him.
He grinned, then stretched across to talk to the girl alongside him.
Theresa studied him. He was at least twenty. He had dark olive skin and long, thick curls that were drawn into a ponytail. A silver stud glinted from his ear.
"Beautiful classic profile," she thought. "He'd belong in Patrizia's time."
Her arms tingled at the thought of her surreal world in the attic fused into her present world. The boy winked at her as the lecturer entered the room.

"Morning, students."

The class was brief, focussed on administration details and practical information. Theresa looked around the room and breathed out audibly.

The boy glanced at her. "Shh"

She flushed.

The class ended and students left for the next subterranean lecture.

Alicia and the curly haired boy hugged. "Ruan, hey man, good holiday?"

"Oh yeah, I worked six nights a week in my Dad's restaurant for two months! Really good."

"Yeah, I worked at Myer the whole break too."

He touched her hair. "Why all black?"

"I went Goth. What do you think?"

"Spanish princess."

"Dork, everyone's a Spanish princess for you. Hey, meet Tess."

Theresa stepped forward shyly and smiled at him.

As he smiled, his nostrils flared, like an aristocratic Palomino horse. "What school you escaped from?"

"Loreto College, except I never went there. Mum and I are living in Sydney for a year, she enrolled me at the school but I hated it."

"Shit teachers?"

"Dunno, I hated the area, the uniforms, everything."

"Passionate girl, I like!" He hugged her and she stood still, unnerved.

Alicia tapped his arm. "Behave, Ruan." She rolled her eyes. "He's Spanish and tragically tactile. But he's not a sleaze, just a dork."

Theresa looked at him. "Did you have a break between school and Tafe?"

"Yeah, I took off after Year Ten, didn't go back for three years."

"Didn't your folks mind? My Mum would go ballistic!"

"My Dad, he's cool. He knew I'd go back, I'd have to work full time in his restaurant otherwise."

"Where is it?"

"Spanish quarter, off George Street."

"Wicked, are you a chef?"

"Waiter, dishwasher, pleb. If my Dad's in a good mood, sometimes I'm allowed to cook an omelette." He stood close to her. "Where're you living in Sydney?"

"At the Rocks."

"Lucky you, that's so hot!" Alicia sighed. "Do you live in a hotel or a pub?"

"Nup, a flat in a terrace. It's cool though. My mum hates it, she's so straight."

"Aren't they all? I'm gonna live in the city one day, or Newtown. It's my spiritual home."

Ruan grinned. "Gothic Spanish Princess in Newtown."

"Shut up, Ruan."

Theresa hung back as she listened to their banter. They walked across to the café and sat down.

She glanced at the terraced houses on Maryanne Street and pointed to them.

"Is Sydney full of terraces? Everywhere I go I see them."

"Not where I live." Alicia scowled. "After Ashfield, it's suburbia, hills hoists, lawnmowers and screaming babies."

"How come you don't go to a regular school then? I did in Melbourne."

"My oldies didn't wanna upset me, I got out of the Clinic early last year and refused to go back to school."

"What sort of clinic?"

Alicia looked away as she spoke. "Anorexia Clinic, I lived in for eighteen months."
"Was it hard?"
"Nup, it was ok, we all understood each other. Like silent sisters, y'know? It's harder being outside."
"But everything's ok now? You're not too skinny?" Ruan felt her waist and Alicia slapped him lightly.
"Absolutely, my relationship to food is one of greed. I'm cured Doc." She stood up abruptly and shouted. "Annabel, Annabel, stop!"

A grey haired woman turned at the sound of her voice and walked across to them.
"Alicia, my muse, how are you? Ruan, give me a handsome hug. Ohh, that will thrill my fading hormones for a week."
Annabel looked at Theresa with clear grey eyes as Alicia introduced her.
"This's Tess, just escaped from Victoria. She's also just escaped from a private school."
"Well done, Tess." Annabel ran her fingers through her short layered hair. "I'm sure you'll love Sydney, our winter's are only half strength."

"It's pretty cool, I haven't seen much though."
Alicia snorted. "Nothing to see outside of Newtown. Bell, are you still there?"
"No, I've just moved to Glebe, you must see my new flat. I've found more retro furniture, real 1950's stuff."
"Rear Window. You need to dress retro now. I'll take you to my fav op shops, I'll be your stylist."
"At my age, Alicia, the retro look would be tragic. You have to be

young to wear vintage."

Theresa looked at Annabel's small, slim frame. She wore jeans and an embroidered vest. From her ears, Indian earrings hung down to her shoulders. A cloth knapsack rested on her back.

"She doesn't need one, Alicia. I do though."

"Done. When do you go back home, Tess?"

"End of the year, I wanna go to Uni in Melbourne."

"Your friends won't recognize you when I'm finished with you." Alicia rubbed her hands together.

Ruan grinned. "Run for your life."

Annabel spoke. "What do you want to study at Uni, Tess?"

"I'm not sure, I love kids so maybe a teaching degree on early childhood."

The older woman winced.

"You don't like kids?"

"Horrible little creatures."

"You don't have any then?"

"Three and four grandchildren. They're interesting when they turn five and even then, only in small doses."

Alicia snorted. "Not even then, I'm never having kids. You, Tess?"

"Lots, I'm gonna have three by the time I'm thirty."

"Ruan, add some sense to this conversation."

"I like kids too, cute to play with and you can pack 'em away in a box somewhere when they get annoying."

"I don't think that'd go down too well with child protection agencies." She sighed. "One of my girlfriends had a baby at twenty. Her life's wrecked totally."

Theresa grinned. "I bet she doesn't think so."

"She doesn't, it's so tragic. She actually loves it," she wrinkled her nose, "the disgusting little toad."

They laughed.

Theresa's heart lilted as she sat with them. It felt like home.

Chapter 8

Theresa ate her dinner as Grace spoke. "Good day at Tafe?"

"Yup."

"What're the teachers like?"

'Wicked."

"I hope that means something positive. Nice crowd of kids?"

Theresa raised an eyebrow. "Mum, some of them are hardly kids. Some of the ladies are grannies, older than you."

"Nice to hear oldies are capable of studying in their declining years."

"Some of them are way chic. You should get a beaded vest and a back pack, it'd seriously update your image."

"I'd look seriously stupid. What subjects did you do today?"

"Same as at school. Mum, I need to call Nick, I'll do the dishes later." She took her plate across to the sink.

"Babes, I'll wash up tonight. You can start your homework after your phone call."

"Thanks, Ma."

Grace watched as the lithe limbs of her daughter vanished into the study and breathed out. "It's a start," she thought, "a better day all round."

Theresa closed the study door and dialled. The interstate beep sounded intimate in her ear.

"Hello."

"Hi, Mrs Vas, it's Tess."

"How's the new school?"

"Actually, I'm goin' to Tafe now, it's great."

A gasp. "How did your mum take it?"

"She's fine, it was her idea. Is Nick there?"

"Yeah, I'll get him. Good luck, honey."

"Thanks."

The line rattled, felt distant.

"Hey you."

"Hi Nick."

"Five days, no call. What's up?"

"Is it? Sorry, it's been hard, I didn't like my new school."

"How come?"

"It felt strange, I'm doing HSC at Ultimo Tafe, in the city. It's way cool, the people are so different. One of my friends is a Goth, she wants to be a fashion designer."

Silence.

Theresa spoke on nervously. "And one of the guys is Spanish and works in town in his Dad's restaurant. He looks like a horse when he laughs."

A low laugh followed and Theresa felt her heart catch in longing.

"Sounds cool. Do you go out with them much?"

"I've only just met them, Nick. Anyway, y'know my Mum would freak if I didn't study every night till midnight. How's everyone at school, who's teaching year twelve English?"

"Same as last year, except Mr Kran's teaching poetry. Should be a weird spin on Eliot."

"Don't bc mean, he's nice. He's just different to the rest of the teachers."

"I know, he loves that French existential crap. Samuel Beckett's psycho spin on the world."

"How's Despina and Tom?"

"Broke up. She's flirting with other guys and he's way jealous."

"She's not a flirt, just a chatterbox. He needs to chill."

"They both do, freezer strength."

She closed her eyes as she listened. "I'd better go, Nick, I've got assignments due next week. Call me soon, huh?"

"You too, miss you."

"How much?"

"Wing span of a jet"

"Nice," she half sighed, "love you. Bye."

"You too. Bye."

She hung up and stared out the window. The wharf's weathered timber suited nightfall's kind shadows.

"Tess," Grace opened the door, "I'm gonna shower and read papers in the lounge. You can study in here if you like."

"Thanks, Ma."

"Makes me feel old when you say that. How's Nick, everything ok at school?"

"He's cool."

"Too much information, babes. I take it from that succinct answer that everything's sunny in his world?"

"Apart from missing me."

"Of course." Grace closed the door softly behind her.

Theresa waited for the click of the handle, then jumped onto the desk and flung the attic latch back. She climbed into the empty, memory filled room. Shadows lapped the chair as she held the diary on her lap. All still in the attic. Mixed scents arose in the air, of oil paint and a hint of lavender. She closed her eyes and surrendered to the diary.

Theresa felt the yearning sensation she associated with Nick grip her heart in sadness. She opened her eyes and looked about. She stood in a quaint room, lit by windows on each wall. The hand-blown glass reflected an icy streetscape below. Eduardo stood next to a window sketching the model ahead of him.

"You're annoyed."

Patrizia frowned and shook her head.

"Now you're more annoyed. Tilt your head to the side and stop fiddling with your cleavage. A hint of breast doesn't hurt a portrait."

She flushed and removed her hand from her throat. "I'm not used to this."

"This?"

"Sitting passively, an object to be painted."

"You thought I'd sketch you running?"

"I feel like a peahen with peacock feathers painted on me. I'm afraid my brown feathers will come through."

"How shall I approach this?" Eduardo murmured as he gazed at her. "You're no French courtesan. How do I paint my peahen?"

"As I am," Patrizia tugged at the blue silk dress. "I'll change into my own clothes and we'll begin again." She hurried to an embroidered screen and Eduardo waited for her.

Theresa inspected him closely. His brown eyes were heavily creased, with lines running from the corner of his lids to his jowls. In repose, he resembled an old court jester. A dab of white powder on his scalp completed the image.

"Done."

Patrizia returned to the chair, her emerald shawl draped across her small frame.

Eduardo stood in front of her. He folded her shawl till it concealed all but her head and throat. He pulled her dark curls to one side and draped them across one shoulder.

Three quarters of Patrizia's face was left exposed, her only embellishment a pair of aquamarine drop earrings.

She breathed out. "That's much better."

"Rubbish, you look like a little French nun. I remember seeing them

run up the stairs of Sacre' Coeur in their black habits. Womanly
flesh offered as a bride of Christ." He shook his head. "I never
understood how they'd forsake passion."

He moved back to his canvas and commenced sketching. "Don't
do the same and live an arid life."
"I've my studies."
"It's not enough."
"I didn't know I'm to be lectured as well as sketched this afternoon."
He laughed. "Touche. I'm an old hypocrite to lecture on morals.
Claudine would laugh at me."
"Was she beautiful?"
"Surprisingly, no. She had an interesting face, all cheekbones and
sharp angles. The Spanish royal women were jealous of her, the way
she carried herself. Her body moved like silk in wind."
He sighed.
"I asked her to pose for me, alone. She refused. Then the incident
happened."
"You must've felt sad."

"I felt the truth of her eyes. It was then I decided it was whores
and courtesans for me, I deserved them."
Patrizia went to speak but hesitated.
"You've the same eyes. Keep still, Patrizia, don't fidget. French
courtesans never fidget."
"What were they like, the courtesans?"
"Marvellous."
"Did you love any of them?"
"No, I had too many."
"I can't imagine you seducing them."
"They seduced me."

She laughed.

"It's true, it's like a court dance. A courtesan would notice me as I stood in a corner and she'd advance. I'd attempt light hearted banter and she'd flirt. Then, we agree to meet. She's more charming, I'm more bold. Within a month, we're lusting away at each other like hares in a field."

He sighed.

"But in the end, the dance palled. Gifts became necessary to keep the rhythm of seduction alive. I needed to breathe again, so I came home to Florence and found new patrons."

Theresa watched as he sketched the outline of Patrizia's face, her fine chin and neck captured in fluid strokes.

"The day I decided to leave Paris, there was to be a winter ball at the palace. I stood in front of the fireplace in the Oriental parlour, warming my hands. The rooms were cavernously cold. From the hallway, I could hear whispers and stifled giggles. Then, in the doorway, I heard the voices of two courtesans. They couldn't see me, I was shielded by a curtain. I listened to them laugh as they held up trinkets I'd given them. I could see cold vapours rising from their mouths, like frozen malice."

He put down his charcoal and rubbed his eyes tiredly. The movement highlighted the myriad blue veins in his hands.

"It was then I decided to come home, to the comfort of my own kind."

"It was a long time ago, Signore, and you're a different man."

"I am, born again in your eyes. Sit by the fire, I've sketched enough today."

Theresa stared out the window, watched carriages clatter past on the snowy cobblestones below. People walked the pavements in their fur coats, shoulders bent against the wind. Patrizia sat on the floor in front of the fireplace and stared at the flames.

"I've news." Eduardo eased his small body into an armchair and lifted a glass to his lips.

"Some of my patrons are returning to England next month and they need a governess for their son." He watched her face as he spoke. "He's a frail boy and needs care. I've recommended you."

She smiled. "Why would I go there?"

"Because the herbal movement's growing in London. Your English is excellent, thanks to your late father's nationality. Lord Millward will try anything to save his son, Jonathon. Go, Patrizia, you'll become independent and respected for your skills. You can further your studies and send for your Mama later. I'll support her until then."

He leaned forward in the chair, eyes focussed on her face. "Take the chance, all you'll achieve in Florence is servitude. I know you want the freedom that a man enjoys as his birthright."

He paused. "Let me help you. Please."

Patrizia moved across to the window.

Theresa was now so close to her, they almost touched. "Go for it, girl." she breathed.

Patrizia stared at the winter landscape in silence. "If you think so." she whispered.

Theresa was stunned at her response. "She heard me," she thought, "she knows I'm here." She moved away instinctively, her body trembling.

Patrizia turned to Eduardo and held up a hand to silence him. "I accept your offer. When I'm able, I'll repay you."

He opened his arms and she ran to him.

Theresa turned away, moved. She touched the windowpane

and felt the uneven surface against her palm. She pressed her face against the glass and felt the cold kiss her lips.

Sounds evaporated as Theresa felt herself imprisoned in a vortex of rainbow colours. She reached out to the glass as she steadied herself. It felt colder beneath her hand. When she turned around, everything was changed. She stood in a grandly proportioned room, objects d'art scattered in careless wealth.

Theresa shivered and walked towards a marble fireplace at the end of the room.

A tall woman with faded red hair sat on an elegant, cream sofa. Opposite her sat Patrizia.

"We'll take you on," the woman spoke in clipped tones. "You'll devote yourself to Jonathon and soothe his ills, even if they exist in his imagination alone. I expect total loyalty. You'll work seven days and have Sunday afternoon free between two pm and suppertime."

"You're most generous, Lady Millward. I'll not disappoint you..." The woman interrupted Patrizia with a wave of her hand.

"Very well, we leave for England in a month. Your appointment will commence upon our last day in Florence. My personal maid will be in contact with you." She moved to the doorway and rang a bell.

"When will I meet Jonathon? I'd like to spend some time with him."

"When you commence my employ."

A uniformed woman approached them.

"Alice, my maid, will see you to the door."

She walked away without a further farewell.

Patrizia was escorted outside and she raised her arms in joy as the door closed.

"Don't go," Theresa whispered. "Don't go, it doesn't feel right."

Patrizia looked in her direction and stretched out her arm.

She whispered. "Please be glad for me, spirit."

Theresa stood, shocked, as a fierce wind encircled her. She wrapped her arms around herself and waited for calm.

Silence in the attic.

Theresa stared out at the sombre night as she leaned against the window frame.

"Help her, Lord" she whispered, "keep her safe."

Chapter 9

Theresa walked with Grace along George Street. As they passed a cobblers tiny shopfront, she paused in the doorway. The smell of leather suffused her senses and her mind caught in a memory. She remembered a little girl perched on a stool in a department store, rubbing the shiny leather of her shoes.

"New shoes, Mama, new shoes."

"Don't lick them, Tess. Yukky!"

"Yummy," she sat on Grace's lap and licked her arm, "you are 'licious, Mama."

"So are you, my ice cream girl. I'm going to lick you away."

Laughter as she scurried away from the arms that embraced her. Theresa could taste love as a little girl.

"Babes, there's our bus, high tail it."

Grace broke Theresa's reverie, pulled her hand as they ran towards the bus stop.

The bus manoeuvred around speed bumps and disorientated tourists with velocity.

"Bastard! He didn't wait for us!" Grace halted, breathless.

A voice called out from behind them. "Melbournite, things not going your way?" Peter approached them, eyebrows raised in amusement.

"Hi, Peter. No, the bus driver didn't wait. In Melbourne, my tram driver would've had a cappuccino on hand for me."

A guffaw in response and a brown hand pulled Theresa's dark hair.

"Good afternoon, pretty girl. How's Tafe goin'? Met any nice boys?"

"Heaps, it's wicked."

"Good choice, Melbournite. I can see your girl's happier."

Grace smiled, bereft of words.

Inside her, a teenage memory of Brighton Baths stirred. The boys at Brighton Beach had walked in a confident swagger of lean bodies and she felt gauche around them. Somehow, Peter had the same effect on her.

"Where're you heading to, so late on a Sunday afternoon?"

"Dinner with my daughter, Willow. She couldn't stay with me this weekend, had too much study."

"Willow? What are your other kids named? Paris? Cherry Blossom?"

"Very funny, Melbournite. Willow's Mum is quite eccentric, hence the name. My son's name is James."

"A handle worthy of a Melbourne child."

"His Mum's worthy of Melbourne. She was a brief interlude in my life, assured me I wasn't worth more than a passing fling and she was wise to me early in the piece."

He grimaced. "It's awful to be analysed so quickly and dismissively as shallow, it wounded me deeply."

"Crap, it's probably true and you deserved it."

"God, you're blunt. Where's the famous Melbourne charm and reserve we hear about in Sydney?"

"Lost them in my divorce. Did you play around on them?"

"The first one, yeah. The second one, nup. I was too stuffed, I had two kids to look after on the weekend."

"Poor man, how tough for you. Still, at least you see your kids."

Peter flagged down an approaching bus and waved the girls ahead of him. "Enjoy some of my Sydney charm, apparently it doesn't stretch too far either."

Grace clung onto the rails as she and Theresa made their way down the back.

"Y'know what they say about back of the bus girls. Melbournite, I

thought you'd sit prudently at the front."
"In Melbourne, courteous women sit at the back of trams and let the elderly sit close to the front exits."

Theresa rolled her eyes and looked out the window. Enchanted newness everywhere. Tourists stood at the war memorial in Martin Place, cameras suspended upwards to record human sacrifice. Exclusive boutiques blurred the mourning space, sales signs indicated a new battlefront behind the obelisk. A harbour breeze teased the flags along George street. Sandstone turned pale orange in the late sun as statues of dead monarchs and explorers looked out on 21st century Sydney.

"Mum, it's our stop. Myer's over there."
The bus driver slammed on the brakes and Grace stumbled as she stood up.
Peter steadied her with a lazy hand.
"Behave, Melbournites. Too much retail therapy sends you blind."
Grace blushed as she exited the bus.
They walked into the crowds and she straightened her shoulders.
"Ok, babes, you need clothes. A couple of skirts, jeans and tops will see you through this year." She walked ahead briskly.
Sales crowds swelled the escalators as they entered Myer.

It was dusk as they left the store and Theresa held up her shopping bags. "Thanks, Mum."
"You need it. Mind you, some of the clothes are a bit psychedelic for me."
Everyone's way chic at Tafe. Alicia's gonna find me stuff at Op shops."
"Dead people's clothes, yuk." Grace looked at her watch. "We might as well eat out tonight. What do you think, pizza at the Rocks?"

"No, let's go Spanish, you can meet Ruan." Theresa tugged Grace. "It's this way."

"OK."

They passed the Queen Victoria Building, it's proportions shadowed in dusk.

Grace stopped as they approached St Andrews Cathedral. "Let's go inside."

"It's Anglican."

"I'm sure a couple of Papists won't cause lightning strikes. C'mon." She walked to the main doors and paused at the entrance. "I love the scent of a church. When I was little, I thought it was how God smelt."

"I can't smell anything."

"It's the scent of candles and church pews. I love it." Grace made the sign of the cross and knelt in a pew, head bowed.

Theresa stood at the back. "C'mon Ma," she hissed. "I'm hungry."

Grace made another sign of the cross as she stood. "Did you say a prayer? I don't feel right unless I say one every day."

"I don't believe in God."

"You just say that because your Dad says it. You'll grow out of it."

"Whatever, c'mon."

They walked out into the early evening. Chinatown and the Spanish quarter submerged past Hoyts cinemas. Theresa stopped on Goulburn Street and scrutinised a row of shop fronts.

"Melbournites!"

They turned to see Peter approach them, his arm around a brown haired girl.

Theresa ran to him as Grace followed slowly behind.

"You've completed your retail therapy?"

Theresa held up her shopping bags as Grace spoke. "Costs the same as psychotherapy, minus the crying."

Peter motioned to the girl beside him. "This is my daughter, Willow. These are my new neighbours, Grace and Theresa. Theresa's the daughter."

Grace laughed. "Charming."

Willow looked out from heavily lidded brown eyes. "Dad always says stuff like that to women. He doesn't mean it."

Peter laughed. "Obnoxious child, your mother's not raising you correctly."

He turned to them. "We're heading to Chinatown for imperial duck and reheated rice. Like to join us?"

"No, we're going Spanish tonight, daughter's request. You're welcome to join us."

"Love to."

Theresa pointed to a faded shopfront. "That's it, Mum. El Passione restaurant."

Peter linked arms with Willow and Theresa and winked at Grace. "Middle aged man's fantasy."

"I'm sure that's what it'll stay, too."

"Ouch, you have a sharp bark, Melbournite."

"My bite's worse."

Theresa nodded. "It is."

Willow grinned at Theresa. "My dad's just the same. He's all talk though."

Peter laughed and hurried the girls ahead. He bent his head in a theatrical flourish to Willow. "Not too many family secrets, don't want the neighbours to know all the dirt. Plenty of time for that."

She smirked.

They walked the neon strip to the restaurant. El Passione had a bohemian charm, the ceiling was intimately low, with exposed beams. Tea lights lit cramped tables, which faced a small area near the swinging kitchen doors. An acoustic guitarist played to a noisy chorus.

The hum of doors and noisy waiters didn't diminish the guitarist's presence. He was about forty five years old, of medium height and strong build.

Grace noticed him as a waiter escorted them to a table. "Gorgeous" she thought.

The guitarist nodded to her and she blushed.

Peter raised an eyebrow. "We like the Latino look?"

"To look at, yes. He's probably an accountant by day."

"Aren't we all?" Peter frowned at the menu. "Red wine is a pre requisite with every dish here, it's heart attack cuisine."

"Hola" a soft call from the next table and Theresa looked up see Ruan approach.

"Hey, Theresa. Is this your family?"

"Ruan, this's my mum Grace and our friends Peter and Willow."

"Good to meet you Ruan. Tess said she's met a nice crowd at Tafe."

"She's a cool addition." Ruan turned to Theresa. "Did you see Alicia at Myer?"

"No, she'd already finished her shift, she doesn't hang about afterwards. Says there's too many weirdos on the train after dark."

Grace smiled at Ruan. "That's your gothic friend?"

"Yeah."

"She must raise a few eyebrows herself."

"Not a bit. Alicia's a princess, even in black."

"Well defended," Grace patted the chair beside her. "Join us if you can."

"Grace's in Latino heaven," Peter grinned, "this would complete her fantasy."

"Very funny" Grace scowled at him as Ruan sat down with an embarrassed smile.

"I'm on a dinner break, I can stay a little while, thanks."

A waiter arrived and looked at Ruan. "Friends from Tafe."

"Are they ready to order?"

Peter closed his menu. "We should have a Spaniard order for us at a Spanish restaurant."

Grace leaned across to Ruan. "Nothing too heavy, my hips don't bounce back so fast."

"Spanish food isn't known for dietary correctness."

"Just do your best."

She sat back and watched the guitarist. His grey hair glinted against the wall as his fingers moved sweetly on the strings.

"Melbournite, nice to see you still appreciate the opposite sex, even if they're bastards."

Ruan looked at Grace. "That bastard's my cousin. I can introduce you to him if you like."

She laughed. "No thanks. I like your style though, Ruan. I'm glad my girl knows you."

Theresa bent her head to hear Ruan above the incessant murmur of voices.

"Your Mum's cool."

"She likes you. Do you have that effect on all Mums?"

His eyes darkened and Theresa caught her breath. "Sorry," she whispered. "I didn't know."

"That's cool. Makes seeing a chick easier if the Mum's on my side."

He stood as a waiter arrived with salad and bread.

"Here's your entree everyone, enjoy. The bottle of red's on the house."

He bent towards Grace. "Good to meet you."

"Come by the flat any time, we're only a bus away. I'd love you to visit us."

He nodded as he moved away.

Chapter 10

Theresa waited on the phone.

"Hello."

"Hi Nick"

"Hey you, it's late. What's up?"

"Nothing, I just wanted to hear your voice. What'ya do this weekend?"

"Not much, studied chemistry and physics. Tom came over and we watched a DVD on Saturday night. It rained all weekend, the usual stuff. You?"

"Same, studied and today I went shopping for clothes with Mum. She met Ruan tonight, we went to his Dad's restaurant."

"The horsey guy?"

"Don't be mean. Yeah, him. It was fun, our neighbours came and Mum drank too much red wine and we had to get a cab home. I think she's gonna be sick tonight, she's lying on the sofa groaning."

"Gruesome. Did she like Ruan?"

"Yeah, kinda. She likes European men, at least until they divorce her."

He gave his low laugh and she felt weightless with love.

"Have Despina and Tom got back together?"

"Nah, he doesn't want to. I don't blame him, she's psycho."

"She isn't."

A silence welled between them.

"What's up, Tess?"

"Nothin, just wondering if you go out much."

"Jealous?"

"Nup, just miss doin' things with you."

"I know, it's a pain. The year'll go quick."

She was silent.

"Tess?"

"Yeah?"

"Oh nothing. It's really late, I'd better go. Call you soon."

"Love you, Nick."

"Yeah, you too. Bye."

"Bye."

A need for physical release inside her, like a coil unwound in her heart, and sent waves through her spine.

"I need..." she muttered. She stood, without conscious thought and pulled herself into the attic. From the window, the Harbour Bridge resembled a steel gateway to the moon.

A strange odour seemed to cling to her pores as she moved across to the chair. The bitter smell affected her balance and she swayed as she sat down. Her eyes stung and she closed them. She heard the sound of a clock ticking.

"Good morning."

Theresa opened her eyes at the sound of Patrizia's voice. She stood at a counter, in a small room lined with shelves. Each shelf held numerous bottles, the source of the foul smell. Patrizia placed a sheet of paper on the counter.

Theresa was surprised by her thinner frame.

"I've a prescription from my Lord's physician. But I think there's been a mistake."

A tall man bent to examine the sheet. "How so?"

"The medicine's too strong for the patient's age. Look."

The Apothecary pursed his lips as he read. "Seems in order. What's the patients age?"

"He's ten next April."

"Bismuth's a good purging agent if his blood's weak. I usually recommend combining it with vivisection."

Patrizia started. "You'll drain him of all his blood if you do that! What Jonathon needs is a course of herbs. I've done much reading since I've been in London on folk medicines. There's a herbalist in Lymestown .."

"Madame," the tone stopped her short. "We've long past the traditions of village simpletons. An apothecary uses scientific rationale."

"Of course." said quietly. "When should I return for the medicine?"

"On the quarter hour." He bowed and turned away.

Patrizia left the room and waited outside on the verandah.

Theresa noticed her hands curl and uncurl as she stood motionless and thoughtful.

"Spirit," she whispered, "I won't allow it. Do you agree?"

Theresa nodded as Patrizia re-entered the shop. "Do it your way." she replied.

Patrizia emerged from the shop, cheeks flushed. "Primitive practices indeed!" She muttered. "At least I don't try to kill my patients." She slammed the door shut, her features tight with anger. Theresa followed, enchanted by the different streetscape. Carriages whittled past, raising dust in their wake. Pedestrians walked briskly, eschewing the elegance of Florentines in their sober colours. Patrizia marched ahead, the glass bottle held tight in her hand. Alongside them, merchant houses intermingled with Georgian terraces. Lush gardens were glimpsed behind iron railings. Theresa glanced at the frigidly cold, overcast sky as she hurried behind Patrizia. They approached a carriageway tunnel. Patrizia entered it first and the sound of her shoes reverberated in the confined space. Carriages clattered alongside them on mossy cobblestones.

Theresa shivered.

Patrizia murmured aloud. "Spirit, you must protect my boy."

Theresa began to shake. "I've had enough," she whispered, "I need to go home." She stumbled and grasped the wall for support. Her fingers slid on the slippery surface and she fell to her knees. The smell of horse dung and wet cobblestones swamped her senses as she stood again. Patrizia was nowhere to be seen and Theresa fled the tunnel. As she ran outside, a different landscape presented itself. The dusty streetscape had vanished and Theresa blinked as sunlight blinded her. Fields surrounded her, rich in an unchecked tapestry of wildflowers. Cows rested under oak trees, as heat rose in the summer air.

Ahead of her, Patrizia's shawl billowed in the breeze. A boy skipped alongside her as they walked down a country lane.

Theresa ran to catch up.

"I see, I see the deep blue sea,
   Won't you sail away with me?"

Theresa's eyes filled unexpectedly at the melody they sang together. "Jonathon, how'll I explain your scuffed shoes to your Mama?"

"I don't care, I've lots more. These are my best shoes now, 'cause I've had fun in them. Do we have to go home today? Can't we stay in the village?"

"No, my treasure. Your parents will miss you."

"Papa won't, he's busy with his club and horses. And I never see Mama anyway."

"She sees you every evening."

"Just to check on what I've done and see if you've missed anything."

Patrizia gave a discreet smile. "Well, you're my guest today, so you can get your shoes as dirty as you like."

He whooped and ran ahead. "Patrizia, I see a puppy!"

He ran into the field and searched the long grass. The blades tickled his nose and he laughed as he sprinted ahead.

Patrizia looked on and Theresa sensed her professional eyes were assessing the frail boy.

A pound of brown and white fur appeared from the meadow and ran towards him.

"You're real!" Jonathon scooped the wriggling pup into his arms and turned towards Patrizia. "Can I keep him?"

"I think he belongs to someone."

His eyes blurred over.

"No tears on this special day! Let's make you well, then you can ask your parents for a dog."

Jonathon let the puppy go abruptly. "They'll say no, Mama hates mess. It won't even be allowed to stay in the servants quarters." He began to walk. "Let's go. I'll walk on the grass, it'll keep my shoes clean."

Patrizia began to sing softly. "I see, I see the deep blue sea."

She ran ahead and linked arms with him and spun him around.

He began to laugh as they shouted: "Won't you sail away with me?"

Jonathon collected a handful of stones and began to throw them. The puppy followed as they approached a hamlet of thatched cottages.

"White washed and with a sprig of thyme on the door." Patrizia murmured. "It's this one, Jonathon."

She knocked on the low door.

"Enter."

The latch opened to a circular room, with high ceilings. At a bench in the centre of the room stood a young man. He was short and slender, with startling blue eyes.

"Mr Seb?"

He nodded. "M'lady."

"I've heard of you in London. I've brought my young charge, Jonathon, to see you."

"A London boy, come here young master."

Jonathon stood up from wrestling the puppy and leaned on the bench heavily.

Seb watched him shrewdly. "Your skin's discoloured."

Jonathon made a face. "I took some disgusting medicine, didn't I, Patrizia?"

"Some bismuth to purge his blood."

Seb murmured. "So young."

"I disagreed but no one listened to me."

"You're the child's aunt?"

"Governess."

"How did his parents feel about your coming here?"

"Lord Millward's desperate for Jonathon to get well before winter sets in. He's agreed to my suggestion of a course of herbs."

"And his mother?"

Patrizia remained silent.

"I see."

Seb smiled at Jonathon. "You can play with Daisy now, she's my daughter's puppy." He continued to observe the boy as he rolled on the floor.

"He didn't swallow the bismuth," murmured Patrizia. "I told him just to gargle it."

"You probably saved his life."

She watched him anxiously. "What do you recommend?"

"Follow me."

Theresa stared about the room, it resembled an exotic botanic exhibition. Roots and herbs hung on white washed walls, seeds and powders filled clay pots that lined the walls. Contrasting aromas suffused the room.

Patrizia scooped some brown seeds into her hand. "We use these in Italy."

"For gout m'lady?"

She laughed. "For lovesickness. The genesis seed can spark love or revive a fading one."

"And its success?

"Complete. It gives a true answer, no more or less."

Seb grinned. "I've never treated anyone for lovesickness. We English aren't so taken with it as on the Continent." He stopped in front of a pot and filled a small bottle with white powder.

"Give this to Jonathon. One scoop of arsenicum album, before breakfast. Continue until he improves and then stop the remedy."

"And a course of herbs?"

"One remedy at a time. I want to see him again in a month."

"Thanks, Seb."

"Thank you. It's the rich Londoners that keep my family, there's no money in farming."

"And the villagers?"

"I treat my brothers free. The Londoner's pay for my philanthropy as well."

Patrizia laughed and produced a velvet pouch. "Let me continue the tradition." She looked about the room "I'll be a herbalist one day, I'm studying in London."

"You're welcome to use my herbs anytime."

"That's so kind. Come, Jonathon, we must leave, our carriage arrives soon. You'll see Daisy again."

Jonathon kissed the puppy's nose. "Don't grow too much while I'm gone."

He skipped alongside Patrizia as they walked to the field.
"Now we've something to make you well, my handsome boy. Hurry, there's our carriage."
Theresa followed behind, absorbed in the quiet rhythms of a country day. From the depths of an ancient tree, an eagle flew upward. Its wing clipped a branch as it soared and Theresa watched as a feather descended lazily from the air.
She walked across the field to collect it. As she touched the grass, the field spun around her. Theresa closed her eyes and waited for the familiar sensation to pass .As she opened her eyes, the harbour glistened in the moonlight from the attic window. The eagle's feather shone in her hand.

Chapter 11

"Guys," Alicia looked up from her salad, "are as much trouble as food."

"Princess, your hair dye has leaked into your brain."

"Not at all, Ruan. My current guy thinks I need fattening up. Do you know any fat fashion designers? Is Leonie Edminston fat?"

Theresa looked at her blankly. "Who's Leonie Edminston?"

"Are you alive and living in Sydney? Ms Edminston is a fashion designer and icon of style, you need to know this."

Ruan rolled his eyes. "A skinny, meatless designer doesn't do it for me. Where'd you meet the new guy?"

"At church."

"What church? You aren't even a Christian."

"I know but it's wicked. Everyone makes mysterious crosses on themselves and dip their hands in water and talk about spirits."

Alicia sighed. "I love crosses."

Theresa laughed. "You have'ta meet my mum, she makes the sign of the cross all the time. Whenever she sees an ambulance or watches the news. She's gonna get RSI."

Ruan spoke softly. "My mum used to make a cross over my body whenever I was in the bath as a kid. She said the holy spirit lived in the bubble bath. Is the new guy Catholic?"

"Mmm and Italian."

"Then his mama will try to fatten you up too." He held Alicia's arm. "Chicken wings into drumsticks in three months."

"He's gotta go then. I need a stylish boyfriend. I'm goin' to Taylor Square."

"You'll come back empty handed, princess. You're the wrong sex."

Alicia laughed at Theresa's face. "Poor girl, she's completely bewildered. We have'ta take her out. Annabel, where can I meet a hot guy?"

Annabel looked up from the table behind them and put her book down. "Good question, where can you meet a decent bloke in Sydney? Any ideas, Tess?"

"How would I know? I've just arrived here."

"I said hot guy, not decent bloke." Alicia snorted. "Are you looking, Bell?"

"It'd be nice if a well adjusted forty year old fell into my lap but it hasn't happened so far."

"You need a toy boy, we'll go clubbing together, Bell. Lots of guys in Newtown."

Ruan whistled. "Lots of weird uni students, y'mean. The place to meet cool guys is libraries."

"You never spend any time in them."

"Cruel princess. Smart guys look for chicks in libraries."

Theresa grinned. "Is that what you do?"

"Yeah but none of the girls I talk to in Sydney fall for it. In Madrid it's easy, you sit in the library reading Shakespeare and chicks fall all over you to talk about it."

Annabel arched an eyebrow. "So you'd actually have to read the play to get a conversation going?"

"That was a drag, but the results, whoa"

Theresa spoke softly. "How long did you stay in Spain?"

"Three years, I lived with my Aunt, my Mum's sister."

"Did it help?"

He hunched his elbows on the table. "I went berserk when Mum died, my Dad couldn't control me. I wanted to die too, some days I thought she'd pull me into heaven, I missed her so much."

"You don't have family here?"

"No one here. I spent a lot of time with my Mum."

Theresa grimaced. "It never goes away, the bad feeling, you just get better at feeling it. When my Dad left I was so shocked, I couldn't speak. My Mum worried I'd gone autistic cause she said I always talked so much when I was little."
Ruan smiled. "We still haven't found Alicia a new boyfriend."
"I'll keep the Italian for now, love those crosses." Alicia stretched her arms out to expose a gaunt midriff. "The perfect man, describe him." She pointed to Theresa. "Go on."

"Um, Nick."
"The Melbourne boyfriend?"
"Yeah."
"Why's he perfect?"
"He makes me laugh, he's got heaps of personality, I feel safe with him."
Ruan nudged her. "Is he handsome like me?"
Alicia rolled her eyes. "You're pathetically vain. Is Nick cute?"
"To me, yeah."
"Means he's ugly as."
"No, he's cute but he's Greek, a bit on the hairy side."
"Got the big Greek nose?
"Kinda."
"Handsome is very important on my list, right at the top actually."
"What else, princess?"
Alicia smiled and the sunlight on her face gave her the appearance of a Botticelli angel.

"Good fashion sense, not straight but a groovy sense of style. Tall, cause clothes don't look good on short guys. Brilliant sense of humour, so girls will envy me when I'm with him. Strong aesthetic sense, so we think alike. Won't criticise me in any way, just adore me. Think I'm perfect."

"Glad you're happy to slum it with the Italian for a while."

"Your turn, Ruan. Perfect girl, describe her."

He glanced at Theresa. "Easy. Sexy, not in your face but subtle. The way she walks, wears her clothes and her hair. Beautiful personality, lots of soul and soft eyes."

Annabel shook her head. "Good you all aim high."

"Bell, it's your turn. Perfect man, describe him."

"I'm thirty years past assessing the perfect man. I want someone intelligent, honest and unafraid. I could rock with that."

Ruan nudged Alicia. "You gonna eat that salad? I've never seen anyone push lettuce so hard around a plate, it'll bleed soon."

Theresa stood up abruptly. "We gotta go guys, English is next. See ya, Annabel."

"Goodbye idealists."

"Meet you there, I gotta go to the loo." Alicia picked up her bag.

Ruan walked alongside Theresa. "What'd I say wrong? the thing with the salad?"

"I don't think we should say anything about the way she eats, I bet her folks are onto her about it all the time."

"Smart you, I'm a dumb bastard I know."

"No you aren't, well maybe just a little bit." She grinned. "Maybe totally."

She ran ahead of him and he raced after her. His long strides caught her at the entrance of D building and he held her shoulders with a mock growl. The sensation of pursuit pierced her subconscious and a childhood memory welled in her heart.

"Play hide and seek Daddy, find me." A child hid behind corn stalks, as she jumped on the soil in bare feet.

"I can smell you, a delicious little bottom and munchable arms."
A deep voice above the stalks. "I can feel you," a foot on the soil beside her, "there you are!"
Laughter as Theresa ran away from him. Stalks pulled her backwards, the sun penetrated the stalks in filtered rays. Glimpses of blue sky as she ran.
"Got you!"
She screamed as his arms imprisoned her and she tried to get free. Theresa could touch love as a little girl.

Ruan looked at her. "Got you."
"Not even close."
He looked up. "D building, such a personal name, do you think it stands for anything? Deadshits? dorks? dangerous?"
"Drop outs?"
"That's us, dangerous drop outs." They walked to the lift. "You have'ta look at the stars with me one night."
She raised an eyebrow.
"No really, it's my fave thing to do."
"Where?"
"Observatory Hill, right near where you live at the Rocks. It's the best, I went there all the time as a kid with my mum. We'll take Alicia along."
"She'll be thrilled senseless."
"Shut up, cynical girl. Let a man take charge." His nostrils flared and she laughed at him.

Chapter 12

"God, look at those old grannies. Trying to score converts."
Alicia ran across the road and motioned to Ruan and Theresa to
follow her. "C'mon, Tess hasn't seen Taylor Square yet."
Ruan stopped in front of the Uniting Church on Pitt Street and
smiled at the elderly women brandishing sheets of paper at passers
by. A white haired lady held his arm. "You look like you love music,
you should attend our concert."
"What's playing?"
"Mozart's piano Quartet No 1 in G Minor."
"Whoa, that's some special guest."
Alicia interrupted them. "We're destitute students, we couldn't
afford the tickets."
"This is God's house dear, he doesn't charge admission."

Theresa giggled at Alicia's dismayed face. "C'mon, Alicia,
this'll impress the boyfriend's Mama. You can tell her you visited
church today."
Alicia glared at Ruan as he climbed the entrance stairs two at a time.
"The best seats are upstairs," the white haired lady called out, "the
acoustics are marvellous, much better than the Opera House. No
need for flying saucer gadgetry to improve the sound here."
Theresa pulled Alicia along. "C'mon, we don't have to stay for the
whole thing."
"No wonder she let us in gratis, check out the interior. It's a dump.
We'll probably get pneumonia free of charge too."
The church had seen better days. It was hemmed in by cheap tourist
shops and steak houses. Inside, dark wood panels and stained glass
windows dominated a lofty, high ceilinged space.
"I see what she means about the acoustics," murmured Ruan.
"Check out the audience," muttered Alicia, "average age eighty.

Cultural pursuits are alive and thriving in the emerald city."

Ruan moved to the back of the church and began to climb the staircase to the gallery. It was near deserted, an elderly gentleman sat in direct line of the stained glass windows at the altar. His bowed head reflected an unearthly sheen of pastel colours.

"He's asleep," whispered Alicia, "it's a sign of what's to come."

"Maybe he listens best with his eyes closed." Theresa sat at the front pew with Ruan as Alicia slid in beside them.

"Maybe he's bored shitless." Alicia nodded to the wooden cross hanging on the central beam of the altar. "Sorry, God."

Below them, a quartet walked out from a door behind the altar to muted applause. They were young and formally dressed in evening wear.

"Probably students from the conservatorium." Ruan whispered.

"Riveting," Alicia leaned back in the pew and took out her nail file, "any time you're ready to go, I am."

The quartet warmed up in a series of scales, the string and piano chords reverberating in elegant disharmony. A young man stood alongside his cello, the height disparity between his small frame and the instrument gave him a childish air. He raised his bow and all signs of youth disappeared. A lyrical sound emanated from his hands and Theresa leaned forward to watch his transformation.

A silence hovered as the quartet positioned themselves. A flutter of programmes as the first strings sounded, then melody filled the cathedral like ceilings. A young woman played the violin, her fair hair caught the light as she moved with her instrument.

Theresa scanned the faces of the sparsely attended audience. A middle aged woman sat with a frail, elderly woman in a wheelchair. The woman moved the wheelchair several times at the demand of the older woman and poured water into a plastic cup. The help was accepted imperiously, as the old woman tapped her gnarled hands on the wheelchair, occasionally knocking the other woman's hands. A corsage of flowers gave life to her sparse white hair. She tapped the woman again, oblivious to all but the melody.

The old man in the upper pew opened his eyes and stared across at them.

Theresa noticed Alicia start and abruptly stop filing her nails.

Ruan leaned forward, transfixed by the music. He nodded in time as the violinist carried the melody, the strings evocative in the reverential space.

Theresa noticed the shine in his eyes as he listened. He smiled at her and she looked away.

"I need air," Alicia leaned across. "I'm going outside." She looked paler than usual.

"You ok? You look upset. "

"It's claustrophobic in here. You two stay, I'm going. I'll see you tomorrow." She stood quickly, knocking her hip on the pew as she turned away.

Theresa tapped Ruan's arm. "Let's go, something's wrong."

They followed behind as Alicia fled the church.

"Hey, slow down." Theresa caught up with her on the pavement.

Alicia wiped her eyes with the back of her hand before she turned around. "That was like sitting in an open grave," she grinned, "way too sedate for me. I need some fresh air."

She walked ahead of them.

"Whoa, can we at least walk in the same suburb?" Ruan called out.

"You need a long rope attached to you, princess."

"Never. Free till I die." Alicia stopped at the lights on Elizabeth Street and waited for them.

"Do you ever sit still for more than half an hour?"

"Never, it's bad for my health."

"I loved that concert," Theresa sighed, "makes me want to play the piano again."

Ruan cocked an eyebrow. "You play? I didn't know."

"I stopped last year, it was never the same after dad left. I kept going for years to make the oldies happy."

"That's a long time to make someone happy."

"That's what I've always done. I didn't want Mum to feel that I wasn't coping or my Dad to feel guilty."

Alicia nodded. "Kids are good at that. They don't want to let on that everything's not perfect. Otherwise, it's all their own fault somehow."

She shivered in the sunlight. "Let's sit on the grass and lizard bake."

They crossed over to Hyde Park and found a sunny spot.

Alicia lifted her skirt to reveal thin legs. "I'll probably burn, my legs haven't seen the sun all summer."

"That's un-Australian." Ruan lounged beside her.

"I try to be. Don't want to be a walking caricature of a sun bronzed Aussie girl."

"God forbid you should want to appear normal."

'Facetious, tragically tactile Spaniard."

"Your insults are getting longer."

They grinned at each other.

"That old guy wasn't asleep. Did you see him stare at us?"

Alicia shuddered. "He looked like my grandfather, the creep."

"Your grandfather was a creep?"

"On a good day," she shivered again in the sunlight, "on a bad day, he was a nightmare." She looked away as she spoke, the black folds of her skirt protected her legs as she covered them.

Chapter 13

Grace finished the report, then picked up her notepad to summarise her thoughts.

Anna dropped a load of correspondence onto Grace's desk and caught her breath.

"That's it," she picked up the notepad and admired it, "the reason you get paid fifty grand a year more than me is because you're a better doodler." She slapped her forehead. "I didn't do that course at business college. Silly me."

Grace leaned back in her chair, an embarrassed smile on her lips. "I should fire you, Anna. You're insubordinate."

"Day one was the time to do that, boss." Anna perched on the desk, "Why are we living in la la land during business hours?"

Grace stared out the window. The grey of the Harbour Bridge was matched by fast moving, dark clouds that tantalized rain.

"There's this guy...." she murmured.

"Do tell. Everything in precise, tasteless detail."

"Only kidding. I do have a funny bloke living in the flat below me though."

"Potential?"

"Zero, two kids to two de factos. Also a self employed artist and a sarcastic bastard."

"How attractive."

"Yeah he is. Y'know, the boy you half liked in school even though you knew he was bad news."

"I married him." Anna's smile rippled outwards. "Fling potential?"

"I don't do flings, Anna. Too Catholic and too conservative. We just banter, it's all I can handle. But you should've seen the Spanish singer I listened to the other night. Scrumptious."

"Potential?"

Grace shook her head as Anna scrutinised her.

"Feel good to be interested?"

"Yeah, it's a bit scary though."

"We're waking up, sleeping beauty. There's something in Sydney water, even though we haven't got much left."

An elegant woman stood in the door frame and cleared her throat. "Grace, Mr Gordon wants to see you in fifteen minutes, to summarise interviewees for Head of Marketing."

"Thanks, Carole."

Anna watched her walk away. "All the botox in the world wouldn't undo my wrinkles."

"Really, you think she's had it done?"

"Absolutely, Carole's been here for twenty years and she looks exactly the same as when she started. She's not a day under fifty."

"I'm a lost cause, my face is frozen in a permanent scream. Too much time spent yelling at Tess. Maybe Carole's got no kids."

"Four, I asked her once."

"Definitely botox then."

"How's the kid?"

"She's happy, at least with Tafe. Things aren't so good with Nick, the Melbourne boyfriend. He's not so friendly on the phone from what I gather. Not that she'd ever tell me, I hear her on the phone to Alicia."

Anna's phone rang. "I'll see if she's here. Your name please. Just a moment," she put the call on hold, "someone called Stefan for you."

"Oh no, my ex."

"I'll say you'll call back."

"No, I'll get it over with. Tell him I'm the best boss you've ever had and the worldwide CEO wants to marry me."

"Could I work that into a future conversation? it might sound a bit forced in one hit."

"Ok." Grace sat up straight as she picked up the phone.

"Stefan."

"Grace."

The silence game commenced. Whenever he called, he waited for her to initiate the conversation.

"Not this time," she thought as seconds ticked away. Her neck locked.

"Ok, what's up?"

"Nothing, just want to know if Tess is OK. Is she enjoying Sydney, liking the new school?"

"Yes to all of the above, except the last one. She hated Loreto College, wouldn't even go a day, so she's doing HSC at Tafe."

"Thanks for letting me know. It's an important year, Grace. I said you shouldn't move her this year. You could've waited till next year."

"Play professional doormat you mean, put my life on hold while everyone around me moves on, you included. I've had enough of that, Stefan."

"I'm not saying don't move on. Just your timing's poor."

"Like you remarrying two weeks after your Mum died? Very poor timing, especially for your grieving child."

Silence resonated down the line. She spoke again, an enforced lightness in her tone.

"Anyway, thanks for calling about Tess. Why don't you call her tonight? she's dying to hear from you."

"Actually, I've been flat chat at work and Sarah's been off colour."

Pause.

"She's pregnant, nearly ten weeks and the morning sickness has been really bad."

Grace nearly dropped the phone. "Well that's news, congratulations! A screaming baby and nappies after seventeen years."

"Don't make it sound so attractive, Grace. We're thrilled and Sarah's family are stoked, it's their first grandchild. We know it's a boy."

"One of each. I'm sure Tess'll be ok with it, just approach it gently. She'll need to know before she visits you at Easter."

"Grace, I was hoping you'd let her know, women handle this stuff better."

"Not this time, Stephan, it's your news. You could always let Sarah break it to her, she's another woman you can palm it off to. Congratulate her for me, tell her I've heard boys don't make you suffer as much as girls do when you're pregnant. I must go, I've got a meeting with the CEO in five minutes. I need to prep."

"Some things don't change, you've always slotted work before personal stuff. Bye, Grace."

The disconnected tone rang in her ear as she yelled into the phone.

"Bastard, prick, stupid shit!"

Grace looked up to see Carole's nonplussed face at the doorway again.

"Don't cross my boss, that's my advice," Anna grinned. "You should hear the stuff she's called me already."

Grace bit her lip as she placed the phone back into the receiver. "Carole, tell Mr Gordon I'll be there in two minutes."

"He's running late too, you've got another half hour. Don't worry about your language, he says much worse when he's on the phone."

She gave a wry grin and closed the door.

"You ok, boss?" Anna walked across. "I didn't realise how feisty you were. You should go out with the Spanish guy, it'd be combustible."

"What do you call me if my ex is having a baby? A step ex?"

"Bloody lucky to be out of it." Anna perched on the desk and resembled a friendly pet parrot with her spiked, short hair. "Remember the sleep deprivation and the early nights?"

"Yeah but remember the beautiful baby smells? The babbling and the gorgeous chubby legs? We don't usually argue anymore, he just goaded me on being thoughtless and it's so bloody untrue. I think of everyone, that's why I have no life. Why am I swearing so much?"

"My wicked influence, people tell me all the time."

Grace sighed. "Who do you go home to?"

"Just me but I have a boy to play with on the weekend. My space is my space but I can fling very well."

She motioned Grace to move forward and she massaged her shoulders.

"Part of the secretarial service, offered in times of extreme stress. Now boss, just let it go. Tess is a big girl and she's lucky she's got you."

"That's so nice. You're a treasure, Anna." Grace closed her eyes to hide tears.

"On a national scale, Gough Whitlam's got nothing on me. Boss, here's the list of applicants, you'd better scan them to refresh your memory." Anna looked at her watch. "Let's have a cappuccino before you go, my shout. I'll be back in five."

Grace stared at the bank of clouds that hovered over the Harbour Bridge and her eyes filled again. She turned away and began to read the document in front of her. Inside her, the tumult continued and she accepted it, unnamed and unquestioned.

Chapter 14

Grace knocked on the bedroom door. "Tess, phone for you. It's Nick."

The silence unnerved her and she knocked again. "Babes, it's Nick." She opened the door.

Theresa lay motionless on her bed as she gazed out at the dusky evening.

"Ok, Mum. Thanks."

"You ok?"

"Yeah, kinda. I've got a bad feeling."

"About Nick?"

"Yeah, he hasn't called me since we've been here. Something's wrong."

"You don't know that, maybe he feels bad that he's never called. C'mon, I'll race you to the study, last one's a Ninja Turtle."

Grace rubbed Theresa's back as they parted at the study door. "Don't worry, babe."

She headed to the window seat and looked up at the ceiling angels. "Protect my girl," she thought, "with all your serendipitous grace." She crossed herself dreamily.

"Nick."

"Hey, what took you so long? I've grown a beard waiting."

"A girl thing. Everythin' ok?"

"Yeah, I just wanted to say hi. How's Tafe?"

"Cool, we've finished our first two topics for English and History. Most of the study notes are left up to us."

"Lucky you, our teachers are at us all the time for assignments. When are you coming down?"

"Easter, I'm staying with Dad and Sarah for about four days. I'll get a tram to your place from there." Theresa searched for a new topic as a silence descended. "How's Despina and Tom?"

"Ok, it's good they're not together this year, it's too hard with finals stuff."

"Sure."

Her words dried up.

"Tess."

"Yeah?"

"We can do the same thing this year, it's not as if we'll see each other anyway. Next year, we'll see how it goes."

"Do you like someone else at school?"

"Nup. You're away, so I don't see the point of calling each other girlfriend and boyfriend. We can start again next year."

"Sure," pause. "Can I still see you at Easter?"

"Hey yeah, all the gang can go out, it'd be good."

Theresa's body curved into the computer chair. "Sure, OK. Maybe we could go to the movies, just you and me."

"Depends on my assignments, I'm always late. Hey, I've got physics tomorrow, I need to read stuff. I'd better ring off."

"Love you."

"Me too."

"How much?"

"Maybe we can do this at Easter, it's more fun face to face."

"Yeah sure."

"Bye."

She stared at the polished surface of the desk top. The smooth newness made her want to scratch it.

Grace opened the door. "All ok?"

"He dumped me."

"I'm sorry, babes."

The phone rang and they both started.

Theresa grabbed the receiver. "Hello? Oh Dad," she waved Grace away, "yeah I'm OK. Tafe's good."

Grace returned to the window seat and scowled at the angels. "No bloody serendipity with you lot." She threw a cushion upwards and the plaster cherubs were momentarily obscured. Gravity asserted itself and the smiling visages reappeared.

"Bastards."

Grace waited until the study door opened and Theresa approached.

"So I'm gonna be a sister."

"You ok with it?"

"Yeah, Mum, it's cute. Dad said not to worry about Nick, he said all Greek boys are ignorant pigs and always stick together."

"Trust your Dad to give such humane, philosophical advice."

"Made me laugh."

"Well that's something. So what did Nick say?" Grace noticed Theresa's wet eyelashes and her heart tightened.

"He couldn't see the point of being together when I'm so far away, he said we'll start again next year."

"But you'll see him at Easter."

"I can't go, Dad says Sarah's too sick for me to stay. I can visit them in late May or early June. "

"You want to talk about it?"

"Not right now, I'll call Alicia. I'm Ok, Mum, it's not forever."

Grace watched her leave, then stuck her tongue out at the angels.

Theresa tried to dial Alicia's number. Within her, a vortex of grief.

She stood and reached for the attic latch, the physical exertion comforting. Clouds obliterated the moon as she sat in the attic chair and clenched the diary.

"C'mon, c'mon I ...."

A shaft of moon escaped its cloud cover and a grey light illuminated the Harbour Bridge. The attic floor reflected it's bitter sheen. It seeped inside Theresa, crept down her throat and unfurled to her limbs. She closed her eyes to hide from the grey.

A sharp wind blew and forced her eyes open. She leaned on a sandstone wall in front of her and gasped as sour air filled her lungs. A congested river lay below her, small vessels skirted large barges wharved on the river. The wind carried an eerie, Greek chorus of moans.

"Why are the voices so sad?"

Jonathon stood alongside Patrizia, his head barely reaching over the railing.

Patrizia caressed his curls as she answered. "They come from the prison barges down there. They hold people convicted of crime."

"Like what?"

"You ask lots of questions."

"You told me to in class."

She laughed. "I did too."

She bent over him. "These are hard times, people can't find work and they're poor. Some of them steal a chicken to feed their families, some a coat to stay warm. For that, they're sent here, to remain at His Majesty's pleasure."

"But that's unfair! They should say sorry and be sent back to their families."

"I agree with you but the law doesn't. Change will come, for now it exists as an ideal in the hearts of good men. It's spinning silently, weaving thoughts of change. God's infinite, he sees beyond our lifetime." She crouched down. "Do you understand?"

He nodded. "When I'm a man, I'll change things."

"Splendid!" She tugged his curls. "Look how tall and strong you've become, Seb's prize patient."

"But I didn't get my dog. Papa said he'd get me one but Mama said no."

She hesitated. "You're healthy and that fills my heart with joy."

He listened to the cries from the barges. "I know that sad feeling, that's how I felt before you came." He looked away.

Patrizia's eyes filled and she wiped them. "But I have something for you to eat!" She felt in her pocket and pulled out a brown seed.

Jonathon watched as it blew across her palm in the breeze.

"It doesn't look nice."

She laughed. "Try it! The genesis seed's good for all men."

He threw it in the air and tried to swallow it as it fell. The seed rolled away on the cobblestones.

"Monkey! I knew you'd turn it into a game. Fortunately, I'm well prepared for cheeky boys." She held out her hand and he swallowed the seed offered to him.

"Good boy, to trust is to learn. Eat, it's full of goodness."

He made a face. "Why don't you eat one then?"

"I will." She swallowed one and he grimaced.

"The things big people eat! No more for me." He pointed to a sailing ship. "Papa said he'd take me to sea when he goes to France. He thinks I'll have good sea legs."

"I know you will."

"Is it close to your home?"

"To Italy? Yes."

"You can come with us! I'll get a dog and we can stay there forever. I won't eat snails though, Papa says they do as a treat. Can you imagine?"

Patrizia moved away from the wall. "Let's head home, your Mama's expecting you home for dinner. I've lots of reading to do."

"Can I read with you?"

"No, your Mama likes to spend the evening with you. Let's go, my treasure"

"I like it when you call me treasure. Did your Mama call you that?"

"No, my Father did. He died when I was younger than you."

"Do you remember him?"

"No."

"That's sad, you don't know anything about him."

"My Mama told me things. Apparently, he called me mouse and said he'd build a giant mousetrap, so I'd never leave him." She sighed. "But in the end, he got sick and left before me."

Jonathon squeezed her hand and they walked in silence.

Theresa bent down and searched eagerly for the seed in the dim light. It had lodged between cracks in the cobblestones. Low pitched wails carried across the Thames and she shuddered and abandoned her search. She ran to catch up with the others as they walked along a street of Georgian terraces. Fire lamps threw long shadows on the sandstone walls.

Theresa felt uneasy as they stopped at the gate of a forbidding looking house.

Patrizia whispered. "Spirit, I'm safe."

Theresa nodded uncertainly and followed them up a set of sandstone stairs. The front door led to a long, narrow hallway. As they entered the terrace, servants were lifting carpets and ornaments and running nervy fingers along marble fireplaces.

Words rose in the air.

"A thief in the house."

"M'lady's furious."

"The ruby brooch is worth thousands of pounds."

A knot formed in Theresa's stomach as she watched the commotion.

Jonathon fled to a small parlour off the hallway, crying. "I didn't steal it."

Patrizia followed the distraught boy. "No one said you did, my treasure. Your Mama's brooch is misplaced, that's all. Come, M'lady's busy this evening, you and I'll read together in the nursery."

His eyes darkened. "She never lets me touch any of her things. I wanted to see if the squirrel would shine in the dark. I put it under my bed but it didn't. Then I heard Mama scream, she knows I have it." He withdrew a jewelled brooch from his pocket and held it out to Patrizia.

"I didn't steal it, honestly. Will they send me to the big ships on the river?" He clutched her.

Theresa stood alongside a red velvet curtain that sectioned the parlour from the hallway.

She heard a rustle beside her and glanced sideways. Lady Millward stood to her left, a vein pulsed high on her forehead as her eyes shone with cat like stealth.

"It's a misunderstanding, I'll explain to your Mama."

Lady Millward swept into the room and Jonathon hid behind Patrizia. The movement threw her balance and she stumbled. The ruby brooch fell from Patrizia's hand like a silent siren.

Lady Millward bent to retrieve it. "I told my husband nothing good would come from the Continent. Jonathon, go to your room, you've been deceived long enough by this woman's character."

Jonathon stared, his lips tried to form words.

"Go!"

He screamed "You don't understand..."

She stepped forward and slapped him across the face. "You don't understand. There are places that bad children go to."

He blanched.

Lady Millward rang a bell and a servant entered the room. "Take Jonathon to the nursery. I may send a policeman to see him."

The two women stood opposite each other, the lie between them. Colour lit Patrizia's face as she stood still. "You'll ruin me with a lie? You heard what he said, I know it."

Theresa pressed her face against the velvet curtain in disbelief.

Lady Millward called out to the servant. "Send for the police, there's a thief in my house. My son's my witness."

She sat on a sofa, her hand gathered the folds of her skirt, let them loose, gathered them again.

Patrizia broke the silence. "Don't destroy the boy, that's all I ask. You will if he has to lie for you."

A clock chimed on the mantlepiece as Theresa began to tremble. She wanted to tear the velvet lie away.

Silent images flickered in front of her.

Patrizia stood on a stand in a courtroom, her hair drawn from her forehead. Her lips moved, the words lost to Theresa.

Lady Millward sat, her eyes piercing, as she gave evidence.

Signor Eduardo sat in a gallery of spectators, his features drawn.

A judge motioned with his gavel for judgement.

Condemned.

Patrizia stood, head bowed.

Theresa screamed and clutched her head. The motion threw her off balance and she stumbled. Silence.

She sat in the attic chair, the diary in her lap. Her past,

Patrizia's past, overwhelmed her. Clouds swathed the sky, folded her heart in its darkness.

"Oh Lord,"she wept, "help us."

Chapter 15

Ruan leaned close to Theresa. "You're really quiet tonight, you ok?"

"Yeah, I'm just hungry."

Alicia spoke. "Then you've been hungry for a month, cause you've been quiet that long. Get over that guy."

"It's nothing to do with Nick."

"Bull. Let's find you a new guy tonight."

"We're not over, just not together this year."

"Yeah, sure"

"What do you think, Ruan?"

His hair hung loose over his shoulders and emphasized his offbeat features. "Tess, I don't know the guy, keep me outta this."

"C'mon, you must have an opinion, you're a guy. What do you think?"

"You're dumped."

Theresa's eyes pricked.

"Was he your first boyfriend?"

She nodded.

"Met at school?"

"Yeah."

Ruan turned to Alicia. "How long's the right time to mourn an ex?"

"In Sydney, depends on the relationship. If you're together more than six months, I'd say four weeks. You can introduce gentle nightclubbing by week four and serious looking by week five. If it was platonic relationship, it doesn't matter how long you were together, I'd be out looking the next day."

She looked at Theresa. "What category are you in?"

"Ah, the second."

"Girl, you're free."

Theresa looked away.

Ruan shook his head at Alicia. "C'mon, princess, help me choose the pizza."

"Classy joint, Ruan, so authentic Italian. Love the red and white checked plastic tablecloths. No wonder you don't have a girlfriend." Alicia grinned. "But you need a library and Shakespeare to snare chicks. Pity you can't order pizza in a library."

"Did I ever tell you I think you're really ugly?"

"Not lately. Hmm,let's see the menu," Alicia read aloud, "vegetarian pizza with mozzarella cheese, seafood with mozzarella, Hawaiian with mozzarella. We're in trouble, the menu's as cheesy as the decor." She stared at the other patrons.

"No wonder Italian's are so fat. You should see my guy's Mama, she's always eating. Then she snipes about how skinny I am, jealous cow. You must be born with a special gene in Europe."

"At least we eat."

"Overeat."

"How does your guy like your smart mouth?"

"He's on the way out, too obsessive compulsive for me, all he does is work on his car. Boring." She leaned over the table. "How 'bout you, how long do you mourn an ex?"

Ruan motioned a waiter across as he replied. "Forever, I love every girl I go out with. I'm shattered when it's over."

"Puppy dog! Chicks love that kinda talk."

She interrupted him as he ordered. "Don't forget to order salad, minus cheese."

Theresa listened to their banter as they waited for their meal. Ruan rested his head on her shoulder. "You ever gonna talk again?"

"Too cute, Ruan. Why don't you be Tess's boyfriend? She's got class, you haven't. You could absorb it vicariously."

"Ouch."

"Here's our pizza, I bags the salad."

"Fun night out with two chicks, one doesn't eat, one doesn't talk."
The girls grinned at each other. Theresa looked at Alicia while they
ate, watched as she cut her lettuce into shreds, nibbled two wedges
of tomato and finally left her plate, re-organized and untouched.

Ruan caught Theresa's eye. "Where do you live at the Rocks?"

"At the back, the Darling Harbour end."

"Your mum was OK about your going out tonight?"

"She had no choice, I've been psycho to live with this week. She's
walked on glass for me, especially cause of Nick and the baby thing
with dad."

Alicia snorted. "Gross to think your parents are still capable of
having sex."

"I don't think my Mum's having sex with anyone."

"How sad. Is your Dad, Ruan?"

"Hope so, he'd never say. He and mum were always together at the
restaurant. She used to sing to her favourite customers."

"What was she like?"

"Cool, she was like, a spiritual romantic, she believed in angels.
Always said I had an angel on my right shoulder, to balance out the
cruelty of the world."

"That's sweet. My Mum believes in daytime television, Oprah's her
angel."

Ruan looked at his watch. "We should go, the viewing starts in about
half an hour. C'mon Alicia, stop stuffing your face."

They laughed.

"Can't wait to see those stars."

"Sarcastic, Gothic princess." He waved their purses away. "My shout."

They waited outside the restaurant for Ruan.
As he emerged, he pointed to a covered walkway. "Start walking, girls." He climbed a set of convict built stairs, two at a time.
Alicia gasped as she reached the top of the first flight and held her hands on her hips.
"You didn't mention exercise was involved in this adventure."
"Nearly there girls, watch out for bats, they grab anything scrawny for dinner."
Alicia stuck her tongue out at him.
They climbed the last flight of stairs and entered a small park. Giant Moreton Bay fig trees were illuminated by street lamps.
Ruan ran across to the grass and lay down. He patted a spot on either side of him and they joined him, giggling. He pointed his arm upwards.

"This is a nothin' sky, you need to be outta the city, hours out before you really see the stars. I saw my first country sky when I went camping as a kid. Mum and I lay on the grass at night and looked for satellites and shooting stars."
He pointed low in the sky. "There's Orion, he's upside down in the Southern Hemisphere. In Europe, he's the other way up. There's his hunting dogs, Canis Major and Canis Minor."
Alicia giggled. "Spoken like a true fanatic. You're gonna end up bald and alone in a suburban house with a giant telescope."
"Y'know, this'd be a good place to murder someone."
"Too creepy for me, space nerd."
He lunged for her and she screamed and took off.

Theresa watched them and her eyes filled. Memory wove down her spine, like an invisible knot that held her in the past.

A party late last year at Despina's, her first as a couple. The warmth of Nick's hand as he caressed her fingers. Outside in the back garden, a kiss, soft at first, then slower, deeper, tongues connected. Hand in his hair, on his neck. Bliss. The hypnotic presence of touch, everywhere.

She sat up, shook the memory out of her.
Alicia screamed as she ran past. "Tess, grab his legs."
Theresa half stood as Ruan slowed to a gait, then charged at her. She shrieked and ran in the opposite direction.
"Tess, over here."
Alicia stood at the base of a tree, her feet entwined in its gnarled roots.
Theresa looped to her left and swerved from Ruan's touch. She ran towards the tree, tipped hands with Alicia, then climbed the lowest branch and pulled Alicia with her.
Ruan whistled from below. "Impressive girl, are you an ex Olympic gymnast?"
He stretched up to touch their legs as the girls sat on the branch.
Alicia kicked him. "You're cheating, we're on bar." She turned to Theresa. "Where'd you learn to climb like that? It was like being pulled by a weightlifter."
"It's a Melbourne thing."

Alicia swung her legs as a harbour breeze lifted her dark hair.
"This is so fun, Ruan. You have'ta organize more of my social life."
"You've no soul."
"I know, let's keep it that way." She raised her arms in the air. "I'm a princess and my knight will arrive soon to take me to his castle. We're gonna live happily ever after."
"Princess, we're a bit time poor to wait for your prince. You'd better get down, our astronomy tour starts in five minutes."

"What, you mean climb down?"

"Climb, jump, chop the branch down with your nailfile, whatever. We've gotta go."

"I can't do that, I've got no physical co ordination at all. Tess, you have'ta carry me down."

"I'm not that strong."

"Why not? I don't weigh much."

Ruan looked up. "We all know that. Look, jump, I'll catch you."

"No, you'll miss and I'll die. This's more dangerous than nightclubbing."

Her hair swirled in the breeze and obliterated her vision.

"C'mon, I'll be your prince, just jump! It's all of a metre down."

Alicia held her arms out melodramatically and dropped into his arms. A chorus of bracelets jangled in the chivalrous night.

"Thank you, Sir Ruan." She curtsied and he bowed back.

He looked up at Theresa. "Your turn, princess."

"It's ok, I'll climb down."

"Please, princess."

Alicia winked at her. "Come on, Tess, do him a favour. He doesn't get to feel chicks up very often, poor space nerd."

"After I rescue her, you die."

Alicia laughed, her skirt billowed in the breeze with the grace of an impressionists brush stroke.

Ruan looked silently at Theresa, arms aloft.

She held her arms out as he caught her and gently put her down.

He ruffled her hair as they walked towards the Observatory. "I'll be your knight any time" he whispered.

Tears close again. "Yeah, thanks."

"This way, girls," Ruan motioned with his hand, "can't miss a single rivetting minute."

They joined the queue at the Observatory and Alicia rolled her eyes at Ruan. "You owe me," she nudged him, "big time."

A line of suburban parents threw sideway glances at her as children jumped impatiently on the pebbled ground. Bats flew overhead with outstretched wings.

Theresa watched them. "It's their eyes," she thought, "their eyes speak differently."

She watched Alicia's cynical eyes throughout the tour, as she walked with the group behind the tour guide. He was an older man and appeared bemused by her presence.

Ruan's eyes were a contrast, they gleamed with a childlike love of astronomy, a passionate knowledge of the universe above them. He peered through the telescopes, asked questions enthusiastically.

Theresa watched them and felt a pull of love for these two disparate friends.

They stood in the North Dome as the guide spun the chain and pointed the telescope upwards.

"We're in luck tonight," he announced, "a half moon is best for seeing lunar craters."

"You'll love this, girls," Ruan whispered, "it's fascinating."

Alicia clutched Theresa. "Hold me up and slap me if I start to dose off." She murmured. "This is gonna be harder than I thought. That old guy's gonna point out every obscure ball of gas up there."

The tour guide continued on.

"We're also fortunate that it's a good viewing night for Mars. Last night was cloudy and the group missed out on all of this. I might run this a bit longer so you can see everything."

Alicia jabbed Ruan in the ribs. "This goes beyond owing me," she whispered, "you're my serf for the rest of my life."

He grinned and turned to listen to the lecture again.

Alicia leaned on Theresa. "I take it back. Don't be Ruan's girlfriend, no one deserves this amount of torture."

Theresa grinned as the guide continued his talk.

"What'd you think?" Ruan turned to Alicia as they later walked away from the North Dome, in the crisp night air.

"I'm speechless, that was the most excruciating two hours I've ever spent. I'm goin' to Taylor Square. Come with me."

"Nup, I'll walk Tess home. I don't want her going by herself in the dark."

Theresa interrupted them. "It's ok, I'll get a cab on George street, it's two minutes to my place from there."

"I couldn't do that to you. C'mon, we'll walk Alicia to the bus stop. She's big enough to look after herself from there."

He linked arms with them as they descended the hill. The rowdy pubs on Argyle Street disconnected the astronomical world above.

They crossed onto George street. "Not too late a night, Gothic princess. Don't take any happy pills."

"Ok, Grandpa." Alicia flagged down a bus. "See ya Monday. Let's do this again real soon, Ruan." She entered the bus and Theresa waved as it drove past.

He walked close to her, his physicality akin to touch. Ruan motioned to the line of two storey terraces past the Garrison Church.

"Those places couldn't be given away thirty years ago. My Dad told me it was a slum."

"I know, Madame Maruska told me."

"Who? She sounds like a clairvoyant."

"She's the lady who owns the house we live in, she lives in the downstairs flat. She used to be a concert pianist."

"Cool. Do you miss Melbourne?"

"Not as much now, it's kinda good to be away. My step-Mum's probably having her whole house sterilised by now, including my dad. Maybe the whole street."

She halted at a street corner. "This's it, we live just down here."

He whistled. "Million dollar you."

They walked in silence to the grey terrace and Theresa stopped at the gate.

"Mum hates the flat. I'd invite you in but I don't know if she'd freak out, specially if she's got her face mask stuff on. She doesn't look good with a green face."

"It's OK. Did you like the tour?"

"It was brilliant." She reached up and kissed him on the cheek. "Thanks."

He gently drew her near and Theresa felt herself retreat.

Ruan kissed her forehead, then let her go.

"Goodnight, Melbourne princess. I hope your angel takes good care of you. See ya Monday."

"Goodnight."

She looked a long time at him as he walked away.

Chapter 16

Theresa stood in the attic. Ruan's kiss marked her forehead, stirred her heart in a love memory. She rested her head on the window pane and watched cars pass over the Harbour Bridge, to nightclubs, maternity wards and suburbia. The sentinel moon kept time with her. She held the book and ran her fingers down its spine. The kiss had challenged her withdrawn emotions. For the first time in a month, she approached the chair.
"I need to know."
Memories welled in her heart, of a mosaic fountain, a billowing emerald shawl, sandstone architecture. Theresa waited and closed her eyes.

A salty sun on her skin, the swell of the sea beneath her feet. Theresa blinked in the sunlight and looked about her. Tall ships lay moored in a pristine bay.
Alongside her, a tall man leaned on a ships rail, staring out at the shoreline.
Island girls walked in languid motion in the port beside the ship. Sailors examined stalls lined with baskets of limes and oranges. A breeze blew a line of scarves into a vibrant flag.
The ships stern was deserted as seagulls cawed on the deck.
The man's face stirred a memory within Theresa.

"Thought you'd wander the port since you're not on duty." Lieutenant Mark Andrews turned from the rail to face a man of middle height. "Lieutenant Dawes, I've stopped at Rio many times. I prefer to travel west of the Brazils."
"To the Galapagos Archipelago? I've never seen it."
"It's full of extraordinary marine life. Giant tortoises, hundreds of years old. The pirates I crewed with last summer ate them for their

meat, the miserable savages. I sailed back to Plymouth to see if any scientific expeditions were looking for crew. And here I am, ferrying convicts to a southern prison!"

"I can't imagine you mixing with pirates."

"I know they don't appeal to your Christian nature, Dawes, but I was heartsick of wars and wanted a break from naval discipline. I've been at sea since I was twelve. And you?"

"I was a couple of years older. And here we are, perhaps sailing into oblivion. Makes me sorry that I've no family to leave behind."

"Me either. I left home before my voice changed. My father was of your kind, he was the pastor of our village."

Theresa studied the two young men. Lieutenant Dawes had an open countenance, his face was unmarked. Mark's was more weathered, the sea had aged him prematurely. At a corner of his cheek, a long cutlass scar joined to his smile. It gave him a lopsided grin, evocative of mischief.

"You must've missed your father, leaving home so early."

Mark spat overboard. "I ran away from home, I never saw my parents again." He looked seawards as he spoke. "I was a cross for my father to bear. He was a learned man, he loved the Testaments and Chaucer. I was no reader, unfortunately."

"I'm sure he loved you nonetheless."

"So much so that he couldn't speak to me. Just spoke to mother as if I wasn't there. One day I left the house and followed the hedge that lined the road out of our village. It was so high, I couldn't see where I was going. It seemed a summary of my life, all was out of reach for me. Miserable scrap that I was!"

"And you ended up in Plymouth, like so many other boys."

"To me it was bliss, the smell of the sea and all that exotic cargo." Mark sighed. "A life without boundaries, or so I thought."

Lieutenant Dawes clasped his shoulder. "There's good work we can do in Botany Bay. Cook wrote of extraordinary flora and fauna. We'll see marvellous things that'll appeal to your naturalist's heart."

"We'll see the backs of convicts and nothing else. At least I will- you've been marked out as a favoured son of the Empire."

Dawes looked around before he spoke. "Is it true what they say of the Lady Penrhyn?"

"That the marines have whores amongst the women to service their needs? Of course. It's easier than waiting for port."

"Poor creatures! We're to protect them and raise them up, not further degrade them."

"That's the line you take? I'm not averse to a good whore, only I prefer to pay for her services in currency, not favours. And this lot, robbed of daylight and dignity, not much to tempt a man."

"But human nonetheless."

Mark changed the subject. "And you, what prompted you to serve on this expedition?"

"Curiosity," Dawes leaned on the rails. "I wanted to see so-called primitive man, free of Christian learning, to see what he's like in his raw state. Does he worship a deity, I need to know."

"You have doubts yourself?"

"None."

"You're a lucky man," Mark spat overboard again, "to have not a doubt in your mind."

The sound of sailors returning to their ship interrupted them and they parted ways.

Theresa watched and waited.

Chapter 17

Mark's eyebrows were raised. "Smyth, does Captain Ross allow this?"

"No." The older man standing beside him gave a waggish grin. "That's why I insist on it."

Mark laughed. "The true sign of a poor commander, when crew delight in disobeying orders. And what's this woman do?"

"Miss D'Agnese? she's keeps the women remarkably well. Without her, the body count would be higher. If it were left up to Ross, victuals'd be reduced and they'd be chained twenty four hours."

"The crew tell me she's got you wrapped around her finger." The surgeon laughed. "She's got my reputation on it, more likely. I'll receive full credit for the low death rate on this voyage. History will fete me."

Theresa listened as the two men talked.

Sailors bustled around them on the deck, their eyes wary.

The surgeon continued on. "Do y'know what I do for the best part of my day? I sketch my natural history finds. Miss D'Agnese tends to the women's needs and we're both content."

"I'm told the crew hate her."

The surgeon looked surprised. "She probably rebuffs them. But you make up your own mind, you've only just transferred from the supply ship to the Penryhn."

"Apparently, the women dislike her too."

Smyth whistled. "It's her educated manner. She's an extraordinary apparition amongst them. I've asked her many times what her crime was but she won't say. The list records grand theft but she won't give her side." He lowered his voice. "Watch out, she's coming our way right now with a patient."

"I'll watch my pockets, more likely." Mark murmured drily as he turned to watch them approach.

"Careful, Bess, the sun's stronger in the tropics. It'll hurt your eyes."

A netherworld creature appeared on the top step of the hold. Her skin was grey in the sunlight, her emaciated frame sapped of health. She swayed on the top step and the woman beside her steadied her. Bess shook her hand off and limped across to the rail. She stared at the tropical landscape with vacant eyes.

"Bess, you need to lie down." Patrizia turned to Surgeon Smyth. "She needs help."

"Lieutenant Andrews will attend you." He patted Mark on the back. "Do everything Miss D'Agnese says. I'll head to bow, there's good sunlight left to complete my sketch. I found the corpse of a brilliant bird yesterday, right at the foothills. I want to capture its colours before it decays." He walked away briskly and Mark stared resentfully after him.

Theresa was shocked at Patrizia's appearance. Her long curls were streaked with premature grey and were tied together with a rag. Tendrils hung over her forehead and softened the high frown on her forehead. Her olive skin was blanched white by months' captivity.

"Lay her on the canvas, please Lieutenant. No, the other side, in the shade."

He raised an eyebrow at her command.

"Lie still, Bess. We've a couple of hours of fresh air to clear your lungs."

Bess murmured. "How'd you extract that bargain from the surgeon? Perhaps you're not as cold blooded as you appear. " She opened her eyes, the narrow slits focussed on Patrizia's face. "We all trade something in the end."

Patrizia's lips tightened but she made no reply.

"Surgeon Smyth left these for you." Mark placed a handful of fine leaved branches in her hands. "He said the natives of Rio used it for seasickness."

"Did he say the name?"

"He did but it escapes me." Mark flushed under her disappointed gaze.

"Where'd he find it?"

He shook his head.

"And how do I use it?"

He stayed silent.

Her eyes twinkled and his discomfort increased.

"Are you sure it was Surgeon Smyth you spoke to and not the ships cook or the cabin boy?"

"I am."

"At least you're sure of one thing."

Bess coughed and Patrizia scooped the green mucus that splattered her dress and threw it overboard.

"Her chest's infected," she murmured. "I need my herbs." Patrizia hunched on her heels and watched Bess with professional eyes.

"Lieutenant, I need my case. It's in my cage, last left as you descend into the hold. Bess also needs her head elevated, I want something to put underneath her. Bring whatever you think is suitable."

She turned away from him and focussed on Bess again.

Theresa watched Mark's face and laughed. "Go, sister." she murmured.

Mark turned away without replying and descended the hold and Theresa followed him.

She clutched the wet rail as she climbed downwards. The lower hull was sectioned into cells, flashes of silver chains were visible in the dark. The smell of primitive hygiene was raw to her senses and she held onto the bars of a rail as Mark walked ahead.

She brushed against a limb and pity rendered her motionless.

A young girl, fettered to a chain, stared out from the bars. Her eyes eagerly sought the source of human touch and she held out a hand. Theresa's heart beat furiously as she backed away.

The girl withdrew into her cell and rocked on the floor in solace.

Ahead, raucous banter followed Mark as he passed the cells.

"Here's a new one."

"Maybe he's here to be broken in. Come here, young stallion."

Mark moved to the last cell and a woman gripped his arm.

"You're on an errand for your mistress. We know her ways, she don't like to go on her back amongst the common lot. The Captains cabin'll do her."

Mark shook off her grasp.

"You show little thanks for her efforts. She tends to your sick."

"She tends to more above deck."

Explosive laughter and some of the women slow clapped as he walked past.

Theresa followed him as he ran upstairs, back to the sun and salt.

"Your case."

Patrizia nodded, her eyed fixed on Bess. "I can't rouse her. Help me turn her onto her side."

Mark bent over and moved the frail woman.

"Thanks, Lieutenant."

Mucus dribbled onto the floor and Mark winced. "I've not got the stomach for what you do."

"Really? you've fought in the wars?"

"Yes."

"Then you've seen blood aplenty."

He smiled ruefully. "But never got used to it though. I prefer the company of animals."

"At least they don't backbite."

They grinned at each other.

Patrizia felt the woman's pulse, then listened to her breathing. She pushed her case away and stared up at the sky.

"Do they always speak to you so rudely?"

Patrizia laughed. "Mostly they don't speak to me at all. They call me Madame W, short for whore. So you see, I prefer their silence."

Theresa watched as pity softened Mark's gaze.

"Do you know how long we'll be at sea, Lieutenant?"

"Three months yet. I'm sorry it won't be sooner for you."

"It'll be easier at Botany Bay." Patrizia looked at Mark calmly. "At least Surgeon Smyth needs me. He's someone I can talk to."

Mark pointed to her case. "That's a fine bag you have."

"Given to me by a fine friend who tried so hard to clear my name. At least my sentence was reduced, I was to be transported for life." She sighed. "In a way, I understand their malice. It's an awful thing to be sentenced to life."

"Will you stay in the Colony afterwards?"

"No, I'll start again in Florence. My Mama needs me."

Patrizia's eyes followed the passage of a gull, as it flew in a series of swoops and cries. "She's gone."

The quiet words startled Mark. "Pardon?"

"Bess. She's dead." Patrizia closed the woman's eyes. "I knew she wouldn't see the day out. God's air is restricted medicine on this voyage but it's all I had left to offer her."

Patrizia stood. "I'm ready to go below, Lieutenant. Thank you that she died free."

Theresa watched them go below. She closed her eyes and waited for the silence in the attic to cocoon her.

"She came here." She breathed.

Chapter 18

"No more crap, Mum."

Grace spluttered her tea. "Pardon?"

"My new motto, no more crap."

"Explain, babes. Are you referring to my cooking?"

"From guys. If Nick thinks he can break it off for some pathetic reason, I don't have'ta accept it. And Dad can see me even if Sarah can't, he should stand up to her."

"I agree but expect to feel differently some days."

"What do you mean?"

"Well, today you feel strongly that you were treated badly. Two days from now, you may feel differently, more forgiving. That's the nature of hurt, it takes different emotions over many days to heal. It's a slow process."

Theresa's eyes filled.

"But," Grace continued, "I've always found anger a good way to propel myself forward! Go girl."

"Thanks."

"I must bolt. Lock the house when you go out and check the windows."

"You mean in case anyone abseils from a helicopter to break into the second floor?"

"This's Sydney. Anything's possible."

"Yeah, yeah, I know. Have a good day, suit."

"I won't, I feel like death this morning." Grace coughed as she left the flat.

Theresa sat down in the sunny warmth of the window seat. She liked this time of day, the flat was half light filled, half dark, as if two personalities lived inside. A modern spirit and a moody,

Georgian spirit beyond the hallway. She loved the feeling of vacillating between two worlds. She took her backpack and headed down the stairs.

"No more crap." she murmured.

"Absolutely." Peter stood on the landing below, looking up at her. "Hey, pretty girl, what brings on the war cry? Have you joined the Salvation Army or is the Melbourne mum being dictatorial?"

"No, she's cool. My boyfriend in Melbourne broke off with me."

"Silly boy. Don't let it throw your studies." He clasped his forehead. "I don't believe I said that, it sounds so old and responsible. I think I'll go smoke a joint."

"Thanks, it won't throw me."

She reached the front door as Maruska approached from the hallway.

"Good morning, cherub. Look at this glorious day! I'm going to the markets at the Rocks, where are you heading?"

"I've got Tafe. What're you looking for at the markets?"

"Just more of what I have, there's always something to rescue there. Come, I'll walk with you to George street."

She opened the iron gate and let Theresa pass through.

"I love your scarf, Maruska."

"Thanks, I'm a throw back to the 1950's era, a hat and a scarf were mandatory to look smart. Maggie Tabberer and all that. It's very old fashioned, I know but I love the graciousness of the era."

"You should meet my friend Alicia, she's loves that retro stuff. It's really hot now."

"Nice to hear I'm fashionable again. We all need a bit of grace in our lives."

"I wouldn't know how to look graceful."

"Nonsense, there's grace in your tall frame, just like your Mum. How's she enjoying Sydney?"

"Ok I guess, she sleeps most of Saturday when I'm studying but Sunday mornings we look around a bit."

"Have you visited the attic again, cherub?" Maruska kept up an accelerated pace as she spoke.

Theresa nodded as she entered the surreal conversation.

"I haven't enjoyed it recently, it's too sad. I think I'll stop going for a bit."

"Don't."

"Why?'

"I stopped going when I was a young girl and finished the tale many years later. Not all the occupants of this house could see the tale, there's a reason why you can. It won't be clear why, perhaps for many years but you are meant to see it. Patrizia called to my heart and I came back."

Maruska's face caught in memories. "There was much I threw away in those intervening years and they won't come back."

They walked in silence down the sandstone patina of Argyle street.

"Don't you love George street? It gets more crowded with tourists each year, I feel like I need a minder to get across the road safely." Maruska stopped at an intersection and hugged Theresa. "I'll leave you here, cherub. Enjoy your day."

"Bye Maruska, have fun." Theresa headed to the bus stop at Circular Quay.

"No more crap," she thought, "and I mean it." The mantra welled in her heart as she caught her bus to Tafe. The gothic gargoyles on the Maryanne street entrance lay etched in frozen motion as Theresa walked beneath them.

"Hey."

Theresa turned to watch Alicia approach from the courtyard, her step subdued.

"Hi, you heading to English?"

"Yeah."

"I read Keats this morning, I hope they've got him in the exam. He's cool." Theresa put her hand on her heart and recited. "Pillow'd upon my fair love's ripening breast, to feel for ever its soft fall and swell."

"I prefer Auden, he's much more my inner landscape." Alicia spoke. "Lay your sleeping head, my love, human on my faithless arm."

"Too bleak for me. Hey, you ok?"

Alicia sat on a low pillar and rubbed the surface absent mindedly with her hand.

"Nup. My oldies and specialist have said that unless I put on two kilos in five weeks, I have'ta go back to the clinic. I'm nineteen, for shit's sake, I can choose for myself."

"I know but what if your choices aren't good or aren't safe? Then what?"

"It's my body."

"Yeah, it is," Theresa hesitated. "So what stops you?"

"This's such an old story, I'm sick of it." Alicia looked away as she spoke.

"It's a control issue, it's my way of feeling in control. Y'know at the clinic, there's endless bloody counselling with the specialists. It makes you feel worse, not better. Sometimes you just wanna have girl talk, not be so serious all the time. I hate it, hate everyone's concern."

"You don't have to talk about it with me, I couldn't give a shit about it. Or about you."

Alicia grinned. "Thanks. I couldn't give a shit about you either." She stood abruptly. "Ruan, hey space nerd! Over here."

Theresa flushed as he approached.

"How are my girlfriends?"

"You wish. We're debating who's the better poet, W.H. Auden or Keats. Not that it's worth much but what's your opinion?"

"Hmm, a profound question, Gothic Princess. I can see why you came to me." He rested his elbow on Theresa's shoulder. "I think better when I'm touching someone."

She laughed and shook him off and he leaned on Alicia.

"You won't reject me, princess. There's no contest, they wrote in different centuries, both of them mad as."

"Guys, you just can't speak about stuff seriously. Make a choice," Alicia held his arm, "or I'll give you a Chinese burn."

Ruan whispered to Theresa. "Who'd you pick?"

"Guess."

"If I have'ta choose, it's Keats. He was cool about love."

Alicia twisted his arm and he yelped. "A pair of tragic romantics, both of you. True love is always tinged black, Auden really got that. Hey, let's move, we're late."

She walked ahead as Theresa followed behind with Ruan.

"She's sick again," she murmured. "Alicia needs to put on weight or she's back in the clinic soon."

"Shit."

"We have to help her, I just dunno how."

He ruffled her hair as they walked on in silence and she didn't move away.

Chapter 19

"Melbournite, you're back before dusk! Have they sacked you?" Grace paused on the stairs of the landing and faced Peter. "I wish they'd shoot me, I feel shocking." She blew her nose. "Bloody flu, you probably gave it to me, I heard you wheezing all week. Germs came through the bricks."

"Poor you, what you need is fussing over. Got anyone to do the job?"

"Apart from an overwrought, cranky daughter, no. It's OK, I just want to sleep, so excuse me, I'm going to bed. If you haven't had it, I don't want you to get it."

"Very noble, Melbournite. It just so happens that I have a spare hour, I've done a draft of a new canvas this morning, so I've earned some time off. Do you have broth in your fridge?"

"Do I look like the kind of mum who'd make broth? Stand over a stove for two hours boiling a chicken to death?"

"I think it's dead before it hits the pot. Except in certain Asian countries, where apparently a fish or animal boiled alive is a turn on."

"Enough of the aphrodisiac peculiarities of Asians. I need sleep." Grace walked past him and sneezed again.

"Melbournite, I'll be right up to feed you, keep your door open."

"Peter, it's ok, I'm not starving, just dying. I need sleep."

"You need broth and I have some, fresh made. Well, it's been in my freezer for about a month."

"How do you come to have broth? It's a European thing, fat, sweaty mamas slaving over wood burning stoves, chewing garlic cloves. My ex mother-in-law as a case in point."

"My second de facto, as another case in point. The only thing I left the relationship with was a recipe for chicken broth. But it's damn fine, so make room in your kitchen."

She sighed.

"Ok, if you insist. The place's a mess and I'm not cleaning up for you. Unless you want to be really useful and vacuum for me."

"Nup." He turned into his flat abruptly.

"I can't even put my pyjamas on," she thought. "Men are a bloody nuisance, even when you're dying. I must stop swearing so much, I'm turning into a wharfie."

Grace searched for her track pants, as every bone throbbed in her body. She headed to the bathroom to brush her hair and stood in the doorway, exhausted.

"I don't care how I look." She thought and walked to the front room and collapsed on the sofa.

"Knock, knock." Peter entered the room. "Ah, the decadent worker bliss of lying on a sofa at 3pm, sick as."

Grace turned on her side. "Space, third shelf in fridge. Close the door on your way out."

"Not so fast, Melbournite. You're gonna drink the soup."

"Please go away. I feel like total crap."

"Yeah, you look it. OK, I've found the microwave and the on button. Your soup will be ready in five minutes. Do you have any noodles? This's really good with noodles."

"Top cupboard, left of stove. Top shelf, back left. Watch out for spiderwebs and daddy long legs, they love my cupboards."

"Says a lot about your love of cooking. God, some of these spiders are ready to die of old age. Grace, you work too hard."

She sat up, surprised to hear her name. "Um yeah, guess I do." She closed her eyes and crossed her legs lotus style as cupboard doors opened and closed around her.

"OK, my little Buddhist, it's ready."

Grace opened her eyes and stared at the dining table. "This is very sweet of you, Peter. I'm an ungrateful cow."

"You can make it up to me later."

She flushed and his grin broadened. "Melbournite, I don't mean sex, you can take me out to dinner."

"What, for a thin bowl of broth and my own noodles? I'll buy you a cappuccino. Is this the feeble charm the ex's complained about?"

"Yup. Good girl, eat it all."

"It's good, really good. You must give me the recipe."

"What for? Would you use it?"

"I don't know, some primeval mother guilt whispering I should cook this for Tess."

"She's a good kid."

"Yeah, she is. My ex's having a baby, she's taken it really well."

"Medical first?"

Grace spluttered her soup. "Don't be smart with a dying woman." She looked at him. "How do your kids get on? Are they a bit thingy with each other?"

"Nah, they're fine. The age gap isn't as big as Tess's will be. How old's your ex?"

"Forty eight."

He whistled. "Poor bastard, all that broken sleep."

"That's what my secretary said too. I don't remember it being that bad, maybe 'cause I only had one or maybe dementia's taken the edge off my memories."

"I couldn't do it again."

"With your track record, you might."

"Nah, I had the golden snip. My fellas can't swim home."

Grace gave a low laugh and her eyes creased.

"That's a pretty laugh you have, makes you look younger. You should air it more often."

Grace flushed.

"Tess blushes just like you. Y'know, I read an article once that a blush was like a mental erection."

"Then I have the most active passive sex life of anyone I know, I never grew out of blushing."

"Go on, tell Doctor Pete everything. What was high school like?"

"Torture. Kids would ask me to blush and I would, on cue. I so never want to be eighteen again, I don't know how kids survive it."

Peter rested his head on long, folded arms. "I bet you were cute. Did you come from a sheltered background?"

"More like barricaded, my dad was so strict. Tess doesn't know how good she's got it. How about you, were your parents bohemian like you?"

"God no, they were country people, I grew up on a farm. My dad was a jack of all trades. My childhood was climbing trees, swimming in dams. Pretty idyllic."

"So I guess you need space, you know, somewhere in a forest to beat your chest on a regular basis."

"Nup, I couldn't wait to leave the country. I arrived in Sydney in 1980 and found Nirvana. First I lived in Paddington, then Newtown. Those decayed, squashed in terraces and workers cottages, I loved them. It felt like home straight away, the pub nights and the wild, eccentric girls. Newtown in 1980 was something else, it wasn't gentrified then. I graduated from East Sydney Art College and never looked back. In the end there was no one to go back to anyway."

He drummed his fingers on the table. "What were you doing in 1980?"

Grace looked at her nails. "I got engaged, I was planning the big wedding."

"The whole year?"

"No, I think I used half of 1981 too."

"Same year as Charles and Di."

"Same fate too."

"Did you have some good times? how long were you hitched?"

"Fifteen years. Having Tess was our best time together. Same old story, if we hadn't married so young, we wouldn't have married at all."

"It's funny isn't it, how those years in your twenties shape you. The essence of who you are is just emerging, then you spend the rest of your life figuring out how to change it."

Grace sighed.

"Something I said, Melbournite?"

"Something you reminded me of. I hope Tess doesn't marry young, I'm glad Nick broke it off. He's too opinionated and she's so starry eyed and naive."

"Like mother, like daughter?"

"Yes, I'd love her to meet a free spirit, someone who'd help her let go."

"Someone like me?"

"I guess, maybe just a bit more stable."

"How can you say that to a man who's just cooked for you? Ungrateful woman."

She laughed and bent down to her soup.

He leaned forward. "Does her mum need a free spirit too?"

"No, she's too old and too settled. She wants to take up knitting and get a cat."

Peter looked at her thoughtfully. "I hope my kids have that carefree time I had."

"I'm sure they will." She looked at his long fingers, paint smudges evident. His lazy grace suffused the room.

She yawned and stretched her arms.

"Melbournite, you need some sleep." He collected her bowl and walked to the sink.

"Please don't wash up, I'll do it later."

"Don't worry, I wasn't going to, my homemaking qualities don't stretch that far. Get some sleep, I can see you need it." He brushed her shoulders with his beautiful hands.

Grace watched him leave. The gentle surf of Brighton beach echoed in her memories.

Chapter 20

Ruan, Alicia and Theresa lay on the library lawn, the mown grass an aromatic, summer memory. Ruan pulled at a blade of grass. "Hey, ladybird! Come here, little girl." He scooped the insect onto his finger and leaned across to Alicia.

She held her hand out and the ladybird made a trail through the fine hair on her forearm. With a distinctive jerk, its wings opened and it flew back to the grass.

Ruan turned to Alicia. "Two kilos, Gothic princess, is that all? You could do it in a week."

"Could we get off the subject of my weight? It's boring."

Theresa shook her head at him but he smiled back.

"No I'm serious, I have the perfect eating plan for you." He sat up. "For breakfast you eat a bowl of porridge, followed by four jam doughnuts."

Alicia giggled as he continued.

"For lunch, two hamburgers and a piece of fruit. Gotta have your roughage."

"Go on, you haven't covered dinner."

"I know, this bit covers your carb's. A plate of pasta with half a kilo of cheese, two bowls of ice cream to finish off. By seven days, you'll be fat as."

"I like it, it's practical and achievable. What'll it do for my health?"

"Bugger all." He flipped open his backpack. "I've got something to start you off."

From a pile of creased notebooks, he pulled out a punnet of strawberries and a yogurt and plastic spoon. "I got this at Seven Eleven, you owe me five dollars."

He held his hand out and Alicia slapped it away. "I'm not paying you if I don't eat it."

"Now watch Theresa," he held a strawberry up, "open your mouth, eat the strawberry. Good girl." He patted Theresa's head and pretended to hold a microphone to her.

"How did it taste? fulfilling? life giving? best meal you've ever had?"

"I feel I've put two kilos on, it was so nourishing."

Alicia laughed.

Ruan waved a strawberry at her. "Now it's your turn, princess."

She pulled away.

"Please."

Alicia sat up and accepted the strawberry. She stared at the redness that stained her hands. The automatic doors of the library sounded a discordant note behind them.

"Ok, thanks."

"Do your best. I'll head off now and get the hamburgers."

"Space nerd," Alicia called out, "don't forget I like my hamburgers served with tomato sauce."

He nodded and walked towards the library.

Theresa watched Alicia's hands twirl the plastic spoon. She went to speak, then stopped.

Alicia pointed the spoon at her. "You do that a lot, like you've got a sensor in your brain, auditing conversation. What were you gonna say?"

"I just wondered how your guy is, you haven't mentioned him lately."

Alicia drew her knees closer and rested her face against her velvet skirt. "This really pissed me off, he dumped me before I had the chance to dump him. I like to be the one to give a guy the flick."

"I wouldn't know how."

"Call Nick tonight, tell him he did you a favour, that you've never had a better time."

"Yeah right. I did call two nights ago to say hi but his mum said he wasn't home."
"Did you believe her?"
"Nup."
"Fat cow."
"She isn't y'know. Fat, I mean, she's a skinny cow."
They laughed.
"My mum would freak if she heard me say that. She's always going on about kindness."
"You're a Sydney girl now. It's survival of the quickest. My guy was a total pain, he criticised my dress sense. Can you believe it? He wears track pants to the movies and I'm the bad dresser. I don't think so." Alicia sighed. "It's hard to pick a guy, they start off so sweet. Was Nick sweet?"
"He's fun, everyone follows him, he'd always pick where we'd go out."

"I like guys like that too. His mum thought I had problems, whenever I came near, she'd go off and cook or speak Italian. I knew she was speaking about me. Bitch."
"Nick's mum would speak Greek in front of me, like I didn't exist." Theresa frowned. "My new resolution is no more crap."
"A crap free life, how easy'll that be to achieve?"
"Dunno."
"No guys worth looking at here, you have'ta come clubbing with me."
"I'm eighteen in October."
"Do you always wait for the right time to do stuff? I've been clubbing since I was fourteen."
"Ever get caught?"

"Heaps but I always had false ID. My oldies never knew."

"Really? Or were they just pretending?"

"Dunno, bit of both I guess. My Dad's OK but my Mum's weird. She's always depressed, always taking tablets. I hate her." Alicia frowned. "I'm never gonna have a boring life in the 'burbs. I'm gonna train to be a designer in London, then live in New York and have my own label."

"Cool, remember me when I'm stuck in the 'burbs with three kids and a mortgage."

"I will, I'll send you designer gear. You'll be the best dressed in your mum's group."

"Not too much black, I don't want to scare the babies."

"Absolute monde!"

They sat on the grass. Beneath them, the microcosmic world of ants built towers amongst the blades.

Chapter 21

Sunlight made the colours of the cove sharply clear. The profile of the Opera House resembled a cockatoo in flight, feathers frozen in white peaks.

Grace pressed her face to a shrub. "Divine! Smell this, Tess, it's from Malaysia. Is anyone around?"

"Mum, do you have convict blood? You're always nicking plants from places."

Theresa glanced at a group of people that approached their path.

"C'mon, leave it. This's the Botanical Gardens, someone'll notice if you're lugging a plant under your arm."

Grace touched the petals as she stood up. "It'd look so nice on our front window sill. I miss having a garden." She smiled as the group passed them. "The gardens here are as pretty as Melbourne's"

"C'mon, I'm over these garden trips, I've overdosed in seventeen years."

"Just like your Dad, he couldn't appreciate them either."

"Smart Dad."

"You'll change, a gene will kick in when you're thirty and you'll be plant mad too. You loved flowers as a little girl."

"Yeah right, hope I remember to pay for them."

"Oh that, I get that from your grandparents. Your grandma loved all the plants in this new country. Whenever we'd go on a picnic to a National Park, she'd take another cutting and put it in the esky. How do you think they ended up with such a brilliant garden? Old fashioned theft, except in those days we didn't know it was theft."

"You do now, Mum."

Grace gave a non-committal smile as she bent down and pulled a sapling from the soil.

"Mum!"

"Shh, everyone will hear you. Keep walking." She looked across the harbour to Fort Denison. "Magical spot, isn't it? Are you hungry? Let's have pizza at the Rocks."

Theresa scowled and they walked in silence along the mellow promenade of Lady Macquarie's Chair. Pelicans bobbed amongst luxury craft in the bay. A Manly ferry blasted its horn as a small boat veered too close. A grand Madame admonishing a novice.

They stopped at the Opera House forecourt and leaned on the rails. The white sails of the Opera House reflected hazily in the heat.

"Mum."

"Yes?"

Theresa rubbed the pebbled seawall. "Did you miss Dad when he left? I don't remember you crying."

"No I didn't."

Theresa glanced at her.

"We were arguing a lot, every night would be another massive fight. Stephan was really unhappy, he was turning forty and I think he felt trapped. You were so little, I worried how the constant fighting was affecting you. Don't you remember that?"

"Nup, mustn't have been too bad."

"It was! Maybe you blocked it out. Anyway, when he left, the house was calm again and it was so much easier to parent. Stephan must've felt the same because we never discussed reconciling."

"That's all I wanna do, get back together with Nick. I miss him, miss talking to him."

"It must be hard, babes. It's not like you had a fight or a chance to outgrow one another. He just broke it off and didn't offer genuine reasons why."

"Well he did, he thought the distance made it pointless this year."

"Don't you think that's a bit selfish? If you're in love, that's an obstacle sure but not a point of dispute."

Theresa moved away from the wall. "Can we go home now? I've got Tafe tomorrow and I'm tired."

Grace kept her tone light.

"Sure, I've got work I can prepare. Now that I'm over this wretched flu, I can think straight again. I bet my desk's stacked with files." She glanced at Theresa's bent head. "Love," she thought, "the great leveller."

They walked through Circular Quay and turned into Argyle street. A cat miaowed at a wrought iron gate, cajoling its errant owner home. Shadows nipped at their heels as they passed the Garrison church.

Shadows followed them within the terrace.

Theresa waited until night, when the shadows connected into a black void and propelled her to the attic. She stared sombrely out the window, aware that she and Patrizia would meet on a shared continent. She sat on the chair, head bowed as if in prayer and held the diary.

Moonlight fell on her, like a benevolent God, as she waited.

An eerie wail sounded and she opened her eyes. A pristine shoreline surrounded her and she recognised Sydney Cove's outline. Trees were felled to within one hundred metres inland, their giant stumps dotted the landscape.

Summer sounds and scents of her homeland. Eucalyptus-scented air, the drone of cicadas and call of kookaburras.

Daub huts and canvas tents lay huddled together as fires burned in the dusk. Bennelong Point lay stripped bare, its future white sails inconceivable in this chaos. Children played on the shoreline and decorated sandcastles with seashells.

Ahead of her, Patrizia walked through the village. Women glanced at her with conspiratorial eyes as they bent over fires. Theresa ran to catch up and Patrizia cocked her head in her direction.

"Spirit, you're here at last. I've needed you."

Theresa followed as Patrizia walked to the furthermost hut.

"Herein."

A tall, bustling woman opened the flap and hugged her.

"It's good to see a smile, Mary."

"Not many thrown your way, I'm sure. Come in, Patrizia. I'll brew some tea."

A small, white haired boy lay on the sandy floor.

"Neddy, my love, how are you?"

The toddler remained motionless and Mary caressed his hair. "He's not recovered fully from his winter cough, we need some of your bush magic."

"Not you too, Mary. Do y'know my new nickname's bush witch?"

Patrizia rolled her eyes. "Still, it's better than Madame Whore."

Mary laughed. "I don't listen to the gossip at the wash tubs. And you've a legion of supporters in the village now, the second fleeters speak of you highly. Surgeon White says it's a miracle so many survived."

Patrizia crouched beside the boy. "Angel child, let's examine you."

She felt his chest and throat. "Cough for me, Neddy."

A feeble response and Patrizia laughed. "Bigger than that! I want a blow me backwards, it's so fierce cough."

He attempted it and Patrizia fell backwards. "You could hear that in London! Nothing wrong with you, Neddy. Mary, let him rest for the week, his chest's clearing. I'm really pleased with him."

She tickled his tummy and he giggled and rolled over.

Mary offered a cup of tea.

"How lovely to drink from a china cup! You spoil me, Mary."

"What do the others offer you?"

"Spite."

Mary smiled gently. "Don't take it to heart, the women resent your pardon."

"I didn't ask for it."

"No, worse than that, Phillip offered it freely in honour of your work. It's clean work too and that riles them more. You walk dainty about the village and they're bent over in lard and sweat. There's no honour for them and their sentences loom long."

"You make me sound so unattractive."

"Not to all. There's the greater rub."

Patrizia laughed. "They can have the militia! I want nothing to do with them."

"Really, not even one?"

"No."

"I see. Well, you've your case to cuddle at night."

"Mary, you're a tease."

"If you did, he'd be happy. Thomas heard Lieutenant Andrews speak of you to Lieutenant Dawes. Such high praise, I'm sure your ears burned."

"They didn't."

Mary smiled and changed the subject.

"Poor Dawes, the militia are greater gossips than the women! They've him married off to a native and living her customs."

"Patyegarang? She's sweet, I've studied bush remedies with her. I think Lieutenant Dawes sees her as a sister, not a lover."

"He won't last long in the colony now. The Governor's sour on him, thinks him too attached to the natives' feelings."

"He'll be a great loss to his friends. I know Lieutenant Andrews loves him."

Mary smiled slyly. "Not that you care if Lieutenant Andrews is miserable. Poor man, rejected by the woman he loves and suffering the loss of a friend."

Patrizia shook her head. "Goodbye, Neddy. Look after your mama. See that she doesn't mix washing and words at the tubs."

Mary laughed.

Neddy tugged at her skirt and she picked him up as she opened the flap. She pointed upwards to the darkening sky. "These giant southern stars amaze me."

"Lieutenant Dawes says the naming of them'll take years." Patrizia hugged Mary, then struck a path towards the village.

A pipe sounded on the shoreline. It blended sweetly with cicada song and the sound carried to the huts. Theresa watched curiously as Patrizia turned and headed towards the music.

Mark sat on a rock ledge as he played, in bare feet and worn uniform.

Patrizia approached him quietly.

Across the bay, Cadigaleans hunted fish and collected oysters. She watched them glean the barren shore, made fertile in their ancient hands.

"I knew if I piped long enough, I'd catch something."

Patrizia smiled. "I'm to add pied piper to your many talents?"

"Phillip thinks I'm a good herder of men. That's not much skill to take back to England, is it?"

"I've heard we may lose Lieutenant Dawes soon."

"He's an irreplaceable loss. I've seen his journals on the Cadigal language, they're extensive."

"You should continue it for him."

He looked away. "I've not his talents. Those hedges are too high for me."

Patrizia bent her head to hear him and Theresa's heart caught as she listened.

"But you love them as much as he does."

"There's a world of difference between us," he spoke. "I left my schooling behind at twelve."

"I'd help you."

"Why?"

"Because no one else'll record their language or habits. I'm afraid it'll be lost one day, the Cadigals are moving further away each year. I'm ashamed we've pushed them out."

His eyes lit up. "I've felt that too! They're clever people, not in our way of thinking but intuitive. Their knowledge of the bush and sea's amazing, they've lived here thousands of years and not starved like us. They're as much a part of the landscape as the kangaroo but soon they'll be gone."

Patrizia nodded. "I've felt it with Patyegarang. It's a shame that Lieutenant Dawes feels his position's hopeless after the raids."

"Mine too. Phillip was wrong to punish the Cadigals for McEntire's death, he was stealing their livelihood."

"That's not the way the Governor saw it."

"To our shame. I should leave too but I'm drawn to this place. Have you travelled to any parts of the harbour?"

"Not yet, I've only been pardoned a week."

"So I've heard. I'd congratulate you but I know in a way it makes your position harder."

She gave a wry smile. "I'm beyond caring. I want to see the river that leads to Rose Hill, I'm told it's beautiful. The Governor's granted me a small plot near there and I want to start cultivating it."
"You're not going back to Italy then?"
"No."
Silence fell between them as laughter and cheers sounded from the village campfires.
Mark pointed upwards. "Look, a star's falling."
A white orb of light spiralled in a graceful arc above them, then extinguished itself.

"I lost her." Patrizia murmured. "My mama died this winter, Signore Eduardo sent me word. I know he cared for her as family but I wasn't there to say goodbye."
"I'm sorry."
She dabbled her hand in a rockpool.
"I accept your offer."
"What offer, Lieutenant?"
"Your offer of writing for me. In return, I'll cultivate your garden for you."
She hesitated.
"Are you worried what people'll say?"
"It's a bit late for that."

"I thought you'd choose a settler husband and mould yourself on Mrs Macarthur."
"Did you?"
"She's much admired. But not by you?"
"She's educated and charming and everyone likes her."
"And?"
"I feel like I'm drowning when I'm near her. She's very tea and piano and has many interests." She sighed "I'm always a

conversation behind and I don't have interests, I have passions. I'm not much of a fine lady."

"You are to me."

Silence between them as kookaburras called in the dense bush.

"I should head back."

"I'll take you out," Mark held her arm, "and show you the coves. They're amazing. Miniature rainforests that grow under giant trees and magnificent sandstone that cradles this land. Remember, you've made me an offer. We English like a good contract, we've built our empire on them."

She laughed and slipped her arm free. "Done. My reputation can't suffer anymore than it has."

"I'll do my best to uphold it. Perhaps Mrs Macarthur can give me pointers."

"Goodnight, Lieutenant Andrews."

"Mark."

"Goodnight, Lieutenant Mark." She grinned and walked away.

He lifted the pipe and began to play.

Theresa saw shadowy figures disperse on the sand as Patrizia headed to the village.

She closed her eyes and waited for the calm of the attic.

Moonlight shone on her as she sat in the chair. The ancient tale of love resonated in her heart.

Chapter 22

Grace looked across at Anna and went to speak, then hesitated. "Boss," Anna looked up, "speak. I feel like I'm watching a silent movie and you're the heroine. Come on, Pickford, what gives?"

"Nothing really, I'm good."

"Is there a reason for this bonhomie?"

"I want to take up belly dancing."

"Won't meet a lot of men doing that."

"True but I'd fulfill a wish I've had for years."

"Good for you, it's time to do something all for yourself. How's the kid?"

"Up and down. You know the mad emotions of love gone wrong. Tess goes through them all in a day, every day. She's killing me."

Anna sighed. "God yes, my current boy gives me grief. It never gets any easier."

"Is it solvable?"

"Well, his mum tells him that I'm too old for him."

"Nice of her. What's his vintage?"

"Thirty four."

Grace snorted. "You do pick well."

"I do. Pity I can't control the relatives."

"So what do you do together?"

Anna arched an eyebrow. "What do you think?"

"Ok, but after the horizontal mambo, then what?"

"Domestics, he stays with me for the weekend, then he's out the door Monday morning."

"Don't you want him for more?"

"No way, I've got limited time and patience with him. Anyway, once he's ready for a family, I'm history. You try looking around, the market share for fifty year old men who are even faintly kindred spirits is abysmally poor."

"I told you, I've never tried. Maybe when Tess's at uni. If I found someone, I'd want him all for me."

"That's the dream, Grace, but this is life. People have families at our age and history. An undamaged, middle aged man would be a miracle. And snapped up fast too."

She bent her head and typed into her keyboard again.

Grace stared out the window as she listened. "That's the sound of my life."

"Pardon?"

"My life's speed and motion, meetings and laptops and busy secretaries. I want something else, Anna, I just don't know what. Y'know, I've caught the bus to work the last two weeks, I wanted a change. I can make a small, safe decision like that but I..."

"Belly dancing's a good start, boss."

Grace nodded as she watched a plane sail into a rainless ocean of white clouds.

"Boss, you've a busy day ahead. Haven't you mastered the corporate trick of looking productive even if you're not? At least pick up a pen and doodle."

Grace grinned and swivelled back to her desk. She dialled home.

"Hello."

"Hi Tess. How's the study day going?"

"Good, if only the phone would stop ringing, I'm trying to read Keats. Dad just called, he said Sarah's better and I can definitely go in June."

"Great, did he have any other news? Is Sarah fat and uncomfortable? I hope so."

"Mum!"

"Sorry, Freudian slip. Can you prepare veggies for dinner?"

"Yeah."

Deep sigh on the line and Grace grinned. "Ok, I'll let you go, overworked child. Hope your study day's constructive."

"Mum."

"Yes, be quick."

"Don't worry, you're busy."

"No, I'm not. What's up?"

"Alicia's sick."

"What do you mean?"

"She's anorexic, maybe she has to go back to a clinic. We don't know what to do."

"Who's we?"

"Ruan and I."

Grace sat up sharply. "What can you do? If she's mentally ill and won't eat, a clinic's the best place for her."

"She's not psycho, just anorexic."

"Babes, it's a mental illness. Alicia needs constant surveillance and guidance, otherwise her organs will pack in."

Grace winced to herself as the silence lengthened. "Sorry, I didn't mean to sound so dramatic. Obviously her family are onto it. Just be there for her, be a good friend."

"Ok, thanks."

"You ok, honey?

"Yeah. Bye, Mum."

"Bye, Tess. Don't worry...."

She hung up and faced Anna's bright eyes.

"Boss, do your family ever ring for light hearted conversation?"

Grace laughed. "I'll start pretending I'm working now."

"Be a change." Anna's click of nails suffused the room.

Theresa stared out from the window seat, the book in her hands. Keats' poetry hung on her, a lovely oral cape.

The phone rang again, sent the rich words upwards to the ears of plaster angels. Whispered of Grecian urns and nightingales.

"It's me."

"Hey, Ruan. You're like the millionth person to ring me."

"And the most brilliant. I was thinking we should all go out to my restaurant one night, y'know, see if Alicia's eating ok."

"Whoa, slow down. My mum says we should back off, just be there for her."

"Wise Mama."

"She's got her moments. I think we should go out but maybe somewhere away from food, like the movies."

"Wise girl."

"Thanks."

"What were you doin'?"

"Reading Keats, I've gotta finish the essay by Friday."

"I've done it, did it last night in the restaurant."

"Did you always do your homework there?"

"Yup. Mum would leave me in the kitchen when I was a kid and I'd sit on top of the dishwasher and do it."

"Was your Mum good to talk to?"

"She didn't really talk to me, y'know, like Aussie mums do, quiet and calm. She hugged me, squeezed me, shouted at me, danced with me. She was the best, like a love tornado."

"You must miss her, I'd cry forever."

He hesitated and Theresa struggled to find words to fill the space.

Ruan spoke first. "I never cry, never have, really. It was like she took my heart, like she owned it and I couldn't cry without her."

"I'm sorry, I shouldn't have..."

"No, it's ok, I like to talk about her sometimes. Makes her real in someone's eyes again."

Pause.

"Hey, so we'll go out next week, we can organise it with Alicia when we see her tomorrow."

"Ok, cool."

"See you tomorrow."

"Yeah, bye."

Theresa walked back to the window seat and picked up the poetry book again. She turned to an ode and curled against the window frame. She stared out the window at the seascape, then abruptly stood and walked out of the flat, into the sunlight of the day.

Away from the shadows and memories.

Late morning. Theresa pushed the gate open as harbour water lapped worn sea walls. She increased her pace.

"Wise girl." The words echoed in her mind, searched her spine to see if they fit.

The sensation of praise warmed her like an internal sun.

"Wise girl."

She walked on, as each step connected her to joy.

Chapter 23

An autumnal wind nipped at Theresa as she sat on the grass at Tafe. She checked her watch and searched the crowd of students that entered D Building. Minutes passed in the cool breeze. She walked to class and scanned the room as she arrived.

Ruan sat at the back and as he smiled at her, she felt a chill in her heart.

They walked towards the lift at the end of class and Theresa turned to him.

"When did she go in?"

"Last night, her mum called me. Alicia's really pissed off, she's worried she'll miss another year of study." His hair cloaked his eyes.

"Can we visit her?"

"Sure, that's why her mum called. We can visit any afternoon, till seven pm."

"Let's go this week."

"I can't, I'm dumped with study stuff and I've gotta work extra shifts at the restaurant. I'll see her soon. You go." The lift opened and he stepped inside. "See ya."

The doors closed before she could answer. Theresa stood in the hall as silence revolved around her. The autistic grief of her childhood whispered into her heart.

Normalcy in her day as she took notes in lectures and selected textbooks from the library. She caught her bus home in the tidal swell of peak hour traffic.

Grief lapping her walk silently. It blurred her thoughts as she studied in the flat.

"Hey, babes, you're quiet tonight." Grace looked up from the sofa, nail polish in hand. She held her left foot up and squinted at her toenails.

Theresa sat at the dining table, surrounded by a pile of textbooks.

"You're usually in the study, why the change?"

"Dunno, I wanted a bit of company tonight."

Grace bent over to her right foot. "I'll warn you now, I'm watching Four Corners in ten minutes, so you'll have a bit of background noise to contend with. How are Ruan and Alicia going with their studies?"

"Alicia's back in the clinic." Tears banked behind Theresa's eyes. Grace walked across on the soles of her feet, cotton buds wedged between her toes.

"Tess, I'm so sorry. Must've been hard when you found out."

Theresa cupped her face into her hands. "Yeah, it was."

"I'll make you a cup of camomile tea with honey." Grace hobbled to the kitchen and Theresa laughed as she looked at her.

"Mum, you look stupid, like a clown."

"The price of fashion. You'll miss her, won't you, babes?"

Theresa nodded.

"Ruan's upset?"

"He looks ok, didn't say much."

Grace reached up to get some mugs from the cupboard. "Men never say much, just fester inside. They usually implode further down the track, by the time we've talked it out of our system." She poured their drinks and shuffled back to Theresa.

"Poor kid, its been hard for you. Y'know, you can defer the HSC this year, if you need to. It's no big deal."

"Mum! I never thought you'd say that. Anyway, I like Tafe and I wanna keep moving ahead."

"Good for you, that's your grandmother's spirit. We come from good depression era stock." Grace sat beside her. "You'll visit Alicia at the clinic? I'll come too if you like."

"It's ok, I'll go on my own. She wouldn't be comfortable with you there." She shook her hair back from her shoulders. "Thanks for the tea."

"But buzz off, I'm busy?"

Theresa nodded as she watched her mum hobble back to the sofa and switch on the TV.

The normal sounds of her life surrounded her, a whistling kettle, tea with honey, words on the page. Pain smoothed away by suburban normalcy.

Grace tilted her feet in Theresa's direction. "What do you think, mutton dressed as lamb with red toenails?"

"Yeah, absolutely."

Graced reached for the nail polish remover. "I thought so, I'll try French Lemon, maybe a subtle colour would be better. I'll never listen to Anna again." She reached for a cotton bud and looked across at the TV, absorbed.

The quiet evening merged to night as Grace switched off the TV at the end of her program. "Don't stay up too late. I'm going to read in bed. Night."

Theresa heard the sound of her bedroom door close. Grief welled within her and she stood abruptly and walked to the study. The attic waited for her.

She closed her eyes and held the diary as the moon cloaked her in a soft light.

A low murmur in her ears and she cocked her head to define the sounds. Whispers slid past her, hid in the walls.

Love whispers.

"Bliss."

Theresa opened her eyes at the sound of Patrizia's voice. They sat in a small boat, navigated by Mark at the helm.

'Good to be away from the Cove, isn't it?" he grinned.

Above them, clear skies bespoke a summer's day.

"Look!" Mark spoke excitedly, "there's a giant stingray. There were hundreds when we first arrived at Port Jackson. There's not so many now."

Patrizia peered into the emerald waters.

The stingray remained motionless as the boat shadowed its enormous span.

"It doesn't acknowledge us at all." She whispered.

"That's why they're easy to spear. Poor creatures, they've no defence against us."

Theresa tried to place the enormous creature. "Are they all gone now?" She wondered.

Mark continued. "The day we arrived in Port Jackson, when you were still below with the women, Phillip ordered extra rum rations for the men to celebrate. I'm sure you heard the commotion. That night, most of 'em were hanging over stern, bringing up the drink. A stingray had settled under the Penrhyn and they tried to harpoon it. I wanted to throw them overboard on the spot. Why is it, when we see a new creature, we have to kill it? Even Reverend Johnson was charmed by the bloodsport."

'Some primitive desire to conquer all God's creatures, I guess."

"The Bible says we're to master creatures, not maim them."

"I didn't think you were a bible-quoting man. Is that Lieutenant Dawes influence?"

"Dawes doesn't quote scripture to me, he knows he'd waste his breath. My father read enough passages to last both our lifetimes."

"Have you forgiven him?"

The question stopped Mark short. "Pardon?"

"You've told me all about him on our trips to Parramatta, what he was like, what your life was like. Have you forgiven him?"

Mark focussed on his steering as they sailed near the riverbank. Water lapped the mangroves, splashed against the gnarled roots. Patrizia sat, legs dangling, bare feet exposed to the sunshine.

"I've not thought about him for years."

She grinned. "But you've talked about him for years."

He looked nettled. "No wonder the women dislike you."

"You're not much beloved yourself."

He snorted. "That's why we're a perfect pair. Who'd spend time with us otherwise? Not the Macarthurs or the Johnsons."

"True. Getting back to your father..."

"Enough Miss D'Agnese. In my way, I've forgiven him."

"I see."

"Two can play court room games," Mark looked at her coolly. "I've heard lots of stories of your mama's devotion. Even of Eduardo. But you never speak of your father, all I know is that he was a British diplomat. What was he like?"

A crow flew overhead, its call echoed in the empty landscape. Patrizia's smile faltered.

"I see," Mark's eyes twinkled. "we've both got our flaws."

She brushed her eyes.

"I'm sorry, I didn't..."

"It's my fault. I'm smart with you, I deserve it back." She looked to the shoreline and her words came out in a rush. "I was seven years old when he died, I should remember him but I don't." She glanced at Mark. "When I was little, I'd tell my aunts about him, all lies and wishful thoughts."

She sighed. "I don't do that now, I prefer to grace him with my silence. It's all I have to remember him by."

Theresa dabbled her hand in the water and Mark looked up at the sound.

"Look, a fish follows us." He smiled. "I did forgive my father. For years, I hated him, felt his praying words were a lie." The boat drifted as he spoke on. "I was in danger many times in my life, thought I'd die before the day ended. Words and passages came to my mind at those times, acted as my shield of strength when I'd none left." He laughed drily. "So you see, even though I can't read or write them, I remember his words. They've saved me many times."

A kookaburra began to sing, the throaty chorus was taken up by unseen comrades in grey trees.

"Beautiful, isn't it?" Mark pointed to the shoreline. "I've heard others complain that it lacks the green of England, that it's drab. But they don't see the subtlety of the landscape, the delicate flowers that grow after it rains."

"I should record your words, not the Cadigals."

"You're mocking me again."

"Not this time."

They stared at each other wordlessly.

Patrizia broke the silence. "Does this mean we'll see you at the Sunday service?"

"You'd hear me snore from the back row. What's it about naval clergy, that only dullards apply? Reverend Johnson holds a special definition of dull all to himself."

She laughed. "He hounds the Governor for a proper church but if they built one, he'd preach to empty pews."

He nodded. "Even convicts discriminate."

"Will you miss Lieutenant Dawes?"

"With all my heart, he's like a brother to me."

"His praying ways don't annoy you?"

"He once said to me that I loved the God of nature. Not many men would see that, Reverend Johnson thinks I'm a savage."

White smoke drifted across from the shoreline. A tribe of Cadigaleans sat near a fire, their leans bodies watchful.

Patrizia rested her head in her hands. "I've often wondered if Lieutenant Dawes loves her."

"Patyegarang?"

She nodded. "If he wants to take her with him and change her Cadi ways. Baptise her, make her a lady and dress her. Y'know, the way men usually do."

Mark laughed. "Men usually want to undress their women but in this upside down world it works in reverse order." He stared at the tribe as their boat drifted past. "I think he loves her but he respects her more. If he took her away, she'd long for this land. The longing would kill her in the end."

"It's sad though."

"Do you have," he paused, "a companion at home?"

Patrizia started at the question. "A lover? No."

"For a girl who likes to ask questions, you can give remarkably short answers."

She laughed. "It's the truth."

"Why? There's some in the marines that'd have you in an instant."

"What of it?" She sat up crossly. "Men are free to travel and work but women must be housebound. And if you're unlucky enough to have your husband die first, the servitude's worse. I'll make my own way, this land's new, we can have new ways of living."

"You might fall in love."

"I won't."
He looked nettled.

"And you, is there a girl in Plymouth?"
He nodded. "And Tenerife and Rio and Capetown. There's safety in numbers."
Patrizia looked annoyed. "Well, you'll head back soon enough. Can't have all those women crying into their handkerchiefs for you."
"They don't use handkerchiefs in their profession." Mark laughed at the expression on her face. "You're an innocent flower."
Her face darkened. "Lieutenant Andrews, I've decided to cultivate my own garden from now on. Thanks for all your past help."

"Really?" He leaned closer. "And look after your patients and live on your own still? It'll be hard to fit it all into a day's work. You'll give up sleep, I presume?"
"Perhaps."
"Well, if you find it too taxing, just look for me at the Cove. I'll have found a woman by then."
"Of course, the only thing constant about men is their fickle nature. I presume she'll be a convict lass, who'll fill your heart with pride at her parsimonious economy. You'll have ten children and she'll force you to go to church in a starched collar to make small talk with the Reverend. Lucky you!"
He glared at her. "Of course I could always marry you, a social misfit scorned by her peers and resented by the militia. That'd bring me equal joy."
"At least you'd feel at home."
"That's right, I would. Will you marry me?"

She stared at him blankly.
"What's the matter, cat got your tongue? 'For a girl who likes to

talk, you can be remarkably silent."

Her hands shook and Mark lifted one gently from her lap. "This hand summarises you. It waves in the air when you talk in your Italian way, it teaches me how to plant seeds by the moon and tides. This hand writes for me and gives my life meaning."

He leaned closer and whispered. "If I love this hand so much, how much more do I love the rest of you?"

Her eyes filled as she shook her head.

"Y'know the night at the cove when we saw the falling star, I realised something. You're my inner constellation, the map of my heart. I could no more navigate my life without you, than I could the sea at night without stars. And you?"

She bent her head and murmured. "I love you too."

"I see. So we love each other. Should we kiss now?"

"I think so."

He inched closer to her face and she raised her hand to his lips.

He laughed. "Oh, I see, it's to be a proper English courtship. You're turning into Mrs Macarthur."

Patrizia didn't reply. She tilted his face towards her and kissed him full on the lips.

"Much better," he murmured. "Continental love's much more to my liking."

"There'll be no more girls in port for you."

"No, Mrs Macarthur."

She kissed him again. "Who?"

"Patrizia."

She smiled. "Are we about to hit the rocks?"

He clambered upwards and steered the small craft hard to port. "I'll need to be a better guide for you, my heart."

Theresa watched them in delight.

Mark pointed to the shoreline, close by. "We're nearly back at the Cove, we're just passing Dawes' observatory."
A figure waved to them and Theresa saw the man was smiling, as if he knew their secret.
In her mind, a childhood quote rose unbidden, as if transmitted across the harbour by that godly man.
"And now these three things remain, faith, hope and love. And the greatest of these is love."

They rounded Dawes point and Mark steered the boat to port. Nearby, convicts pulled logs across the soil, their clothes wet with strain. Supervisors languished in the heat.
Theresa felt whispers tremble near the cracked earth.
"Witch."
The whispers reverberated in her senses, disoriented her.
She closed her eyes and waited for the attic chair to reclaim her.
Love and fear, so intimately connected. Theresa stood and rested her head against the window pane. The glass burned like ice on her forehead and cooled the unsettled thoughts of her mind.

Chapter 24

Theresa looked out the window for a familiar swirl of black velvet.

The bus driver turned to her. "Neutral Bay, miss."

"Thanks." A breeze rose up as she alighted from the bus.

A girl waved at her from across the road and Theresa stared at her. "Hey!"

Alicia clutched at her throat as Theresa crossed the lights. "C'mon, I need coffee and a cigarette."

They hugged awkwardly.

"Check out the coffee shops," Alicia snarled as she walked past, "so nicely suburban. They're feral."

Theresa grinned.

"This one's decent, it isn't Newtown but the staff's cool."

They entered a café of steel grey tones. Elegant mums feed croissants to toddlers, who clutched teddy bears and balloons.

Alicia scowled as she reached into her pocket.

"Can you smoke at the Clinic?"

"Yeah, it isn't prison, they can't stop me."

"I can't believe you're wearing jeans and a tee shirt, no Goth black."

"I don't wear it there, it's a part of my life I don't wanna share. The best part."

"You look better."

Alicia took a drag. "Yeah, if I put on a couple of kilos, I can stay as a day patient and get some life back."

"You must miss your freedom."

Alicia blinked and Theresa spoke softly. "Sorry, we don't have to talk about it, I just wanna know you're alright."

They sat silently as a black clad waitress delivered their

cappuccinos.

Alicia stirred her froth, pushed it over the sides of her cup.

"No, it's ok, my Mum doesn't talk about it at all. She babbles on about everything else when she visits."

Theresa felt her throat tighten. "Ruan says hi."

"Will he come?"

"Guys, they're not good at this stuff."

"Nup, they're not. I called my ex and he said his mum was right, I had too many problems."

"Bastard."

"That's what I said," Alicia drew back on her cigarette. "My therapist, Jan, says I use food as a way to control my life. Y'know the crappy bits, like shitty guys."

"Maybe we all do stuff like that and don't know it."

"Yeah, but you don't try to kill yourself." Alicia gave a rueful smile. "Jan's nice, she makes lots of crappy jokes but she doesn't patronise me like some of them do."

She drew back again. "I got banned from group therapy last time I was here, they said I was too subversive. always leading the other girls in a thinness competition."

Alicia tapped her cigarette on the window ledge. "I did, I was always the skinniest, they were way jealous of me. We'd compete, see who'd weigh less at the next meeting." She leaned her head on her hands and looked out at Military Road. "I'm studying feminist therapy with Jan. Mum's scared I'll turn into a lesbian."

Theresa laughed. "Sounds cool, feminist therapy!"

"Yeah, it's all about female and male power issues. I wanted to take up boxing with it but I've gotta put weight on first." She stared at the brown stains in her cup.

"I'm not taking any pills this time, they make you feel really psycho.

The pills make you put on weight, not good weight, bad weight. I felt like I was turning into my Mum. Jan's good that way, she listens to me." She sighed "Fashion's probably not the best career choice for me, everyone's obsessed about skinniness and perfection. It feeds the other obsessions that follow on." She looked away. "I just wanna get past it all."

"You will, you'll be the next Naomi Wolf."
Alicia looked at her watch. "I've gotta go, I only got half an hour leave this time."
"I'll walk you back."
"Ok, just to the entrance, you don't have'ta come in." She waited as Theresa paid, then led the way down Military road.
They turned into a quiet street. The road sloped down to reveal the azure harbour in the distance. Frangipani and wattle trees lined the foreshores.
"Is it a nice place?"
Alicia gave a strange smile. "That's not a word I'd use. It's controlled, it has to be."
She pointed to the well preserved cottages in the street. "Aren't they depressing? Filled with boring women wearing Laura Ashley and gardening gloves. They're all members of Friends of the Botanical Gardens and Taronga Zoo, boring as shit."
Theresa laughed. "Not my style either."
"I'm gonna move out of home when I'm finished at Tafe."

A young woman strode past them with a jogging pram, a dog leashed to one side.
"Sad," murmured Alicia, "too sad."
They grinned at each other as Alicia stopped at a side street. "It's down here. You go back up the hill, you can get a city bus anywhere on Military Road."

"I can meet you next week, I've got a half day on Thursdays."
"Cool, yeah. See if you can drag Ruan along. I'll see if I can get afternoon leave, maybe we can go to the movies."
"I'll ask Ruan."
"Ok. I've gotta go. See you, Tess." Alicia hugged her, a flash of black hair enveloped Theresa and then she was gone. She disappeared behind a high fence, shaded by native trees.
Theresa passed the row of prim cottages as she walked up the hill. Dusk hovered in the autumnal air as she reached Military Road.

....

Grace knocked on Peter's door.
"Melbournite, you've come to repay my great kindness to you?"
"I just wondered if you had time for that cappuccino? Tess is off visiting a pal."
"So you thought you'd sneak a visit in too and repay a debt at the same time. Good time management."
Grace stared at him, defeated. In her mind, a gauche teenager stumbled over the sand at Brighton Beach, her full chest spilling out of a shapeless cheesecloth dress. Boys whistled at her as she walked past shyly. She shook her head to clear the memory.
"Yes, that's me all over. Would you like to go?"
"Nah, it's too close to dinner time, don't want to spoil my appetite. Come in for a drink though."
She hesitated and he looked amused. "Now what's she thinking, I'll owe him for a drink and soup? Career women don't like to feel obligated, what will she do?"

Grace clenched her teeth. "I'd love to."
"Gin and tonic?"
"No, that's a depressive's drink, got any scotch?"

"Yo, practically a cellar full, untouched. Just the smell of it gives me a headache. Why do people always give men bottles of scotch? Every bloody Father's day, every bloody Christmas. You always been a scotch girl?"

"It was all my Dad had at home. We used to have a nip together on winter evenings, to take the Melbourne chill off."

"Bet Ma didn't approve."

"Ma didn't know." She glanced around the lounge room furtively.

"Just stare, Melbournite. You don't have'ta be polite here."

"Thanks." Grace walked past the rows of canvases stacked on the floor. "Some home office. Doesn't Maruska mind the paint stains?"

"I think she likes 'em. She's quite Bohemian herself."

"So Tess tells me. My girl just adores her." Grace crouched down. "I like this one, it feels melancholy to me."

Peter stood at an art deco cabinet as he poured a full measure of scotch. "Just that one? There's a whole flat full of 'em."

"No, this one best. I like the structured lines of the girl's face. I thought you didn't do portraits?"

He crouched beside her with their drinks. "She was some girl, a barmaid in Noosa. People are always something, wanting to be something else. She was studying to be an actress."

"Showed you her lines, did she?"

He laughed. "Yeah. God, you must think I'm seedy."

"Not a bit, I've always admired uninhibited people, specially other women. Who buys your paintings? Do you have regular clientele?"

"Story there. True artists don't have regular clientele, unless they're fashionable or dead. Especially dead. Crap artists have regular clientele 'cause they're happy to mass produce."

He held his drink in the circle of his long hand. "I exhibit and take pot luck. It works for me."

"Brave you, I couldn't do that, I need to have a regular income. I'd go spare otherwise."

"I'd like to see you spare. How many scotches would it take?"

"You wouldn't, I have a filthy temper. My ex once offered to buy me a block of wood to chew on when I was angry."

"Did you accept?"

"Nup, wouldn't have been strong enough. He wasn't good to argue with, Stephan would withdraw and sulk if we needed to discuss something. I had to play twenty questions to clear up an issue. Couldn't stand it in the end."

"How does the new wife cope?"

"Don't know, don't care. Not my problem any more."

Grace walked slowly around the room. "You like aboriginal colours in your landscapes, where'd that come from?"

"My neighbours, when I was a kid. They were part aboriginal, really creative people. The dad, I never knew his name, would dig up clay soil and use it to sculpture and paint. I used to watch, I loved those colours."

Grace spoke. "I had gorgeous neighbours when I was a kid. Mr and Mrs Rush, very English, very cultured. On weekends, they'd have high tea on their back patio and sometimes invite me over. I was the little migrant kid, I felt so honoured to go to their house. I'd wear my best party dress and absolutely stuff my face with cakes. They always pretended not to notice." She took a sip of scotch as she spoke again.

"You're lucky to have the gift of creativity, I so don't have it."

"Really, not even in your little finger?"

"No, just a green thumb but all plebs have that."

"Well that's art, that's expression."

"No, it's cheap therapy." She emptied her glass and Peter whistled.

"Top you up?"

"Knock me unconscious. I'm a one glass screamer but thanks, this was fun. You must let me do something for you."

He grinned and she laughed loudly.

"Whatever, maybe I'll cook you dinner."

"With daughter to protect you?"

"Or we could go out for dinner."

"Much better. With daughter?"

"Without."

"Even better. Melbournite, this could be the start of a beautiful friendship."

She flushed. "Casablanca."

"The best. Let me see you home."

He opened the door and switched on the hall light. "Try not to stagger up the stairs. Don't want Maruska to think the barmaid from Noosa is visiting again."

"Goodnight, Peter."

"Here's lookin' at you kid."

Grace sighed as she climbed the stairs.

Brighton Beach was never very far away.

Chapter 25

"Hey" Ruan crouched down beside Theresa "how's Alicia, shitty about being back in?"

She looked up blankly. "Not thrilled but I think she knows she needs to be there." She motioned to a chair. "Sit down, lots of Shakespeare close by."

"I hate libraries, I can only study with noise around me."

"You told me, on top of the dishwasher."

"Yeah. Let's go for coffee, I wanna hear all the news." He picked up her backpack. "Please."

Theresa closed her book and followed him outside to the courtyard. "Ruan, you seem edgy."

He shrugged. "I guess she'll be out in a couple of weeks."

"Nup, she's gotta go up two kilos before anything will change. I'm seeing her next Thursday, we thought maybe we'd go to the movies with you."

"Yeah, I couldn't handle the hospital bit."

"Ruan, it's not a hospital, it's a clinic. Alicia said it's ok, just really strict."

"She must be going demented, I would." He drummed his fingers on the café counter, then shook a cigarette from his pocket.

"I didn't know you smoked."

"Sometimes I don't know what to do with my hands."

A café staff member pointed to the door and Ruan grinned.

"That was a big success."

He waved Theresa's money away as he paid for their cappuccinos. "Next time."

"There's never a next time with you."

"It's the Spaniard in me, some chicks get really aggro about it. Think

I'm a sexist dog."

"I don't."

"I know." He hugged her and Theresa felt him tremble. "Let's sit on the grass, it's still warm." Ruan handed her the cappuccino and as their hands brushed together, he held hers fast.

"Do you think she'll die?"

Theresa tried to withdraw her hand but he didn't release it.

"No, I don't. Alicia's got too many plans, she's too smart."

He let go of her hand abruptly.

"You ever smelt death?"

She shook her head.

"It's in hospitals, an antiseptic, sterile smell. Just flick a switch, you turn off a life."

A breeze rose up and he shivered. "When you go outside again, it's like the sun's lying to you. I hate that smell."

"Ruan, it's not like your mum."

She held his arm. "Alicia'll be fine, it's not like she's pretending she's ok."

"Yeah." He rolled over onto his stomach and his hair spilled over his shoulders.

"You must've loved living in Spain, getting away from it all."

He pulled at a blade of grass. "Madrid's a different world."

"Lucky you, my folks haven't taken me anywhere."

"Maybe you haven't needed to run anywhere, like Alicia and I have."

He stirred his cappuccino and Theresa grinned.

"It'll be an iced coffee before you drink it."

"Yeah." He glanced at her. "You really love that Melbourne guy, don't you?"

She flushed. "Well, it doesn't matter anymore, he's not interested."

"You might meet someone in Sydney."

"That's a great idea. Then Mum and I will leave in December and I'll be stuffed again."

"You could stay in Sydney."

"I'm all Mum has. I think she stayed on her own all these years because of me."

"She's free to fall in love again."

She smiled. "I gave her a really hard time when they separated. I heard her say on the phone once when she thought I wasn't nearby, that I sucked all the energy out of her."

"Go Tess."

They laughed.

"But," he continued, "you can't be her excuse to stay single forever."

"Are you playing psychiatrist?"

"No, just asking the hard questions."

She grinned and hugged her knees. A shadow lengthened on the grass, darkened their sunny nook. Ruan shivered and gulped his drink. "I miss Spain at this time of year."

"You must've seen a lot of it in three years. "

"Nah, I worked mostly, my aunt's not rich. I waitered a bit, but I got sick of the American chicks cracking onto me. They dropped their tips if I flirted at the table with them. Like it was enough of a favour! Then I worked at a hotel as a bellboy. The old American ladies told me how darling I was and they tipped me heaps. And some of the old American men."

"Gross."

"I just shrugged it off. Americans are definitely weird."

"Your aunt must be sweet."

"She's a character. Aunt Ester's a tour guide, she showed me around the city on my days off. She said Madrid was like a woman's heart and I had to honour it."

Theresa raised an eyebrow and he laughed.

"No, I don't know what she meant either, she always said a lot of mysterious stuff. My Uncle died young, I think she never got over him."

"Sad to think she's lived on her own ever since."

"No way! I think she invented toy boys, she has them hanging off her arm. Aunt Ester believes in destiny. I think it makes crap easier to accept if you can blame it on fate."

They laughed.

"Did you have a girlfriend in Spain?"

"No one serious," he smiled. "I wasn't into commitment. My life felt surreal, even the light was different."

She smiled sweetly. "So you saved your serious girlfriends for Sydney."

"Yeah." He stood. "I'd better go, if we see Alicia next week, an afternoon session would be better for me."

"I'll call her and let you know."

"Cool. See ya."

"Thanks for the cappuccino."

He broke into a run.

Theresa emptied his drink onto the grass. His restlessness was infectious and she headed to the bus stop. Late night shoppers disappeared down escalators like city rats.

People spilled onto the pavement outside pubs at the Rocks. Ties loosened and words flowed, the asphalt a thread of social renewal. Theresa walked on, immersed in her thoughts. "How could Alicia not get well?"

She let herself into the flat and headed to the study. She unpacked her books and gazed at the attic latch. "Not now." She drummed the desk with her fingers and the motion made her look back to the piano.

She walked across, lifted the lid and pressed the keys. The warm tones ricocheted around the room. She opened the music book to an unknown piece and tried to connect the notes. Pleasure swelled in her.

"I miss this," she thought, "my other language."

Memories of childhood sauntered into her mind.

She remembered sitting on her father's lap, her small fingers on antique ivory keys. "Careful, Tess, this piano's precious. It belonged to my Daddy."

"Play, Daddy." She hit the keys and his arms encircled her. The notes of Frere Jacques filled her heart.

"Daddy, you're the best piano player in the world."

Theresa could hear love as a little girl.

She played on. Joy and grief, the primary notes of love, reverberated in her heart.

"Tess, is that you?"

She stopped.

"Hey, it's so good to hear you play again." Grace put her shopping bags down in the doorway.

Theresa closed the piano lid. "It doesn't mean anything, Mum. I'm not having lessons again."

"It doesn't have to, I'm just so pleased you were playing." Grace beamed as she headed to the kitchen. "Green chicken curry for dinner, just give me an hour. I'll leave you, I know you've got an assignment due tomorrow." She closed the door.

Impulsively, Theresa pushed the attic latch back and climbed in. She looked out at the moody landscape and cradled the diary as she sat and waited. Wind whipped harbour waves into the seawall as seagulls flew past.

A heat source crackled low at her feet and she glanced down. She sat in a small cottage, almost bereft of furniture. The only plentiful resource, a collection of wood stacked near an open fireplace.

"Are you sickly in the morning?" An older woman stoked the flames as she spoke.

Theresa watched her hard silhouette and shuddered.

"More like all day long! I can't look at food." Alongside her, Patrizia answered and Theresa noticed her fuller shape.

"Mark's worried I won't have the strength to carry the baby full term. Even Mary says I'm too small for seven months."

"Mary's a fool."

"She isn't, Kathleen. She's been a great friend to me."

"A hoity toity marine's wife, of no use to anyone. Not that she mixes with us."

"Perhaps you just misunderstand her, Mary's quite shy."

"Quite proud, more like it."

The words stifled the air and Theresa sensed Patrizia's unease.

"Do you think I look well?"

Kathleen crossed the room and knelt in front of Patrizia. She felt her abdomen with red, calloused hands. "It's low, a boy I believe. You're small but many women are with their first. I've delivered over a hundred so I know what I'm saying."

Theresa studied her face. It matched her rough hands, pockmarked with deep lines and grooves.

Patrizia smiled. 'That's reassuring. Mark thinks I'm the first pregnant woman in the world."

As she spoke, the front door opened and a gust of harbour air dispersed the room's warmth.

"Good evening, ladies." Mark crossed the room. "Kathleen, have you convinced this disobedient woman to listen to her husband? She should knit by the fire and grow fat."
He rubbed Patrizia's abdomen. "I thought of another example. A bustle worn backwards. Or should that be frontwards?"
"You can sleep under the stars tonight."
Mark winked at Kathleen. "I'm trying to describe Patrizia's new shape. What I meant to say was Madonna like."

Kathleen collected her grey cape.
"I won't meddle in your fight. Why you choose to live on this point, Lieutenant Andrews, I'll never understand. The harbour winds are freezing in the winter. Patrizia'll find it hard to nurse the baby and keep it warm. You should've stayed in the village."
Mark escorted Kathleen to the front door. "It's not even a mile to the village and we both like to be near the Cadi people and the observatory."
"I've said my piece, you do as you like. Goodnight." She gathered her cape closer and stepped out into the night.
Mark and Patrizia looked at each other, then burst out laughing.
"She intimidates me."
"But she's the best midwife in the colony Mark. I think babies are too frightened of her to be difficult at birth."

He stroked her hair absent-mindedly. "I've news."
"Do tell. Governor Grose has promoted you to Captain and we're invited to the Macarthur's ball?"
"Not quite. But I'm released of duty and granted a hundred acres at Parramatta, with convict labour to cultivate it."

She clapped her hands. "But do you want to resign your naval commission? I know you love the mapping expeditions."

"We've some river frontage. If I'm restless, I can go walk about with the Wann-gals for the winter. I'll return to you in the summer."

"You can return to England, more like it."

He laughed and kissed her throat.

"That's nice. You've missed a spot here."

He covered the hollow of her throat in kisses.

Theresa walked to the front window and looked out. The shoreline of the Rocks was lit up by countless bonfires. A group of soldiers surrounded a large fire and Theresa could just make out the red lining of their uniforms in the blurred pane.

A figure in a grey cape stood between them. She extended her hand and a soldier grasped it.

Theresa flung the front door open and ran in the direction of the fire. The group had dwindled to a few civilians warming their hands. Theresa turned and ran back to the cottage. "Don't trust her," she screamed, "don't trust Kathleen." Her foot caught against a rock and she fell heavily. "God," the southern stars spun above her, "oh God, enough."

The images went black as she lay unconscious.

Chapter 26

A kookaburra sang to her, his chest inflamed with song.
Theresa lifted herself gingerly from the ground. Her head throbbed
and she leaned against a tree.
"What do you use this for?"
She walked in the direction of Patrizia's voice. Bush surrounded her,
salt and eucalyptus pervaded her senses in blinding sunlight.

Ahead of her, two Aboriginal women shucked oysters as Patrizia
and Mark sat alongside them on a rocky shoreline.
Patrizia held up a yellow root in puzzlement and one of the women
pointed to her breast. "Berewalgal."
The Aboriginal woman repeated the word in her soft, guttural tone.
"It's for breastfeeding women!" Patrizia cried. She pretended to hold
the root over a fire.
"Gore? do you heat it?"
The woman took it from her, rubbed it on Patrizia's breast and
pointed to her swollen belly.
Mark laughed at the expression on her face.

"It's startling how direct they are. We're so trapped in our
mannered ways, they catch us out in their simplicity."
Patrizia grinned. "Mrs Macarthur wouldn't approve, she'd not have
someone touch her breast publicly."
"Or privately, I'd say."
Patrizia laughed. "We're being very unchristian. Lieutenant Dawes
would be ashamed of us."
"He was a more gracious man than I. Like you, I fumble in polite
society, even our bush version. I'm at home with the Cadigaleans"
Patrizia sketched the root in her journal. "I think it's used raw,
perhaps it's a balm."

A flock of pelicans circled above, then dived and expertly skimmed the waters. The Cadi women watched intently, then began to sing:
"No tu lu brie law low ne lie
Gnoo roo me, la tie, na tie, na tie
No tu lu brie law low ne lie
Gnoo roo me, la tie, na tie, na tie
Tar wane nolie lar rah wuo."
Theresa listened to the song and her heart ached at the loss of this ancient tribe.

Mark lay on the rock, long limbs stretched out to the sun. He nodded to the women as they fell silent. "Beriadwarin, thank you."
"Wanadyu inea." The women stood abruptly and walked into the bush.
"Why do you think they left?" Patrizia closed her journal and stared after them.
"They no longer desired our company. It's as if they know their life's changing forever." He stroked her hair. "Our cottage's nearly ready, we can move in as soon as the baby comes."
"I can't wait to be away from the Cove."
He kissed her hand. "Let's head back, you've done enough translating. I want you to rest after your appointments in the village. It's only a month now."

"I'm more tired this week."
Mark offered his hand and they made their way to a canoe resting on the sandbank.
Theresa climbed into the back as Mark helped Patrizia get in.
"I'm glad no one from the Cove saw us." Patrizia frowned.
"Don't worry, they think we're both mad as March hares. A match

made in an asylum."

She grinned. "Well, I can understand them thinking that about you."

"Be careful I don't tip you overboard. Mysterious things happen to disrespectful wives."

"I know my place, Mr Macarthur."

"Remember that and we'll get along fine."

She laughed.

Sweat stood out on Mark's forehead as he paddled against the current to round a point. Theresa recognised the outline of Mrs Macquarie's Chair, as yet pristine. The timber settlement approached. The sandstone permanence of Macquarie's governorship was years away yet the village had an aura of stability. Canvas tents fortified by determination and bush wattle.

He winked at her. "Your hair curls in the breeze. If my hands were free, I'd kiss you."

"In this canoe?"

"Yes."

"Publicly?"

"Yes."

"Shamelessly?"

"Yes."

"What would Mrs Macarthur say?"

"She'd rap my knuckles with her fan, God bless her."

"I must buy myself a fan, since I'm about to become a respectable Parramatta matron."

Mark pulled into shore and lifted Patrizia onto the sand. "Don't be long. I'll get flour and rice from the storerooms while I wait for you."

"I'll walk home, Mark, the weather's milder of an evening."

"As you please, Mrs Independence."

She blew him a kiss and turned towards the huts.

Theresa followed behind as the afternoon sun threw shadows on the ground.

"Spirit, you're near." Patrizia whispered. "I've missed you."

The words pierced Theresa's heart.

A blond boy ran past on the sand and Patrizia called out to him. "Neddy, look how you've grown."

He looked at her briefly, then scampered away.

A dark haired woman waved to her from a nearby hut.

"Mary! how's the new cottage?"

"Beyond words. Four walls and two window panes are my new idea of heaven. I wanted to burn the canvas tent when we moved here but I couldn't stand the waste."

Patrizia laughed. "I know, I felt the same when we moved to the point."

"When do you leave for Parramatta?"

"When the baby's settled. We're eager to go."

"Kathleen's your midwife, I hear."

"You don't sound happy."

"No, she's capable." Mary leaned closer. "Be careful, I've heard she's tight with the militia."

Patrizia rubbed her abdomen instinctively and Mary forced a smile. "I'm selfish, worrying you like that. I'm sure it'll all be fine." She hugged her. "Go, make sure you're home before sunset."

Something in her voice tugged at Theresa heart. She walked protectively alongside Patrizia as they turned back to the village.

Chapter 27

It was dusk as Patrizia finished her last consultation. Women kneaded dough and gutted fish near open fires. They glanced up as Patrizia passed by, looked away without acknowledging her. Hazy glimpses through the smoke of red lapels and militia men.

"Let's go," Theresa urged, "it's getting late."

Patrizia clutched her case as she quickened her pace.

They reached the last hut near the turn to the Rocks point and Theresa's heart pounded. A group of guards lay sprawled on the ground near the provisions hut.

"Witch." The word rose from behind smoky embers, infecting the air.

"Hurry." Theresa was beseeching now, the smell of cheap rum nauseating to her.

A soldier followed them, the jeers and whistles of his fellow marines ringing in the dusk.

Patrizia's breath was anguished now. "Spirit, protect me."

Theresa stared at the deserted Rocks streetscape. The cottage lay a mile away and the few shops that existed were closed.

Patrizia leaned against a shopfront and pounded the door.

Theresa glanced upwards; a sign above the shop proclaimed it to be of royal patronage. The elegant seal was ironic against the roughly painted premises.

"Witch!" The shout followed them.

Patrizia screamed and ran down a long laneway that bordered the shop.

"No, don't go down there!" Theresa caught up with her. "It's deserted. We'll run to the cottage!"

Patrizia looked in her direction. "Spirit, I'm afraid. Help me."
Theresa felt her tremble and knew Patrizia wouldn't be able to run.
She gently guided her to an open doorway at the back of the shop.
An earthen smell arose as she peered down to examine a newly
excavated cellar. From the stairwell light, she could see kegs
scattered on the floor.
"Hide down there. I'll be back."
Patrizia followed her unearthly command and began to descend the
stairs.

Theresa ran back up the lane.
The marine staggered into view. He paused at the laneway and
peered down. "Witch, I'll have you yet. No lieutenant to save you
now."
Theresa lunged at him and pummelled him with her fists.
He stood upright, oblivious to her presence and she screamed in
frustration.
"Oh God," she screamed, "help us!"
She ran.
Bird calls and ship horns sounded in blurred confusion to her ears as
she ran to the point. A woman from the village had wandered to the
shoreline to collect driftwood.
"Mark, help us!" She flung the cottage door open and Mark started
in surprise.
"Patrizia, where are you?"

"She needs you." Theresa was sobbing incoherently and she held
his arm.
"Is it you, spirit? She's told me of you."
"Yes," she urged, "we need you."
"Where is she spirit? Lead me."
"Come."

She pulled his arm and began to run. He followed her till they reached the deserted premises.

Mark stared at the laneway, puzzled.

"Down here." She pointed.

He stood motionless and she pushed him.

"Hurry!"

A scream sounded and Mark sprinted down, Theresa following behind.

"Witch?" the marine swayed on the stairs in front of her. Patrizia crouched behind a keg at the furthermost corner of the cellar. She gasped as sharp pain stabbed her abdomen.

"You need more than one man, Italian women always do." He followed the sound of her uneven breathing. "C'mon, whore."

Patrizia stood and hurled her case at him with force.

The metal clasp hit him on the forehead and he jerked backwards.

"Devil's spawn, you'll pay!" He lunged at her, struck her across the cheek.

She fell against the earthen wall, her hip knocking against a keg.

"Please, leave me alone!"

He laughed. The mirthless sound reverberated against the walls.

Mark ran down the stairs, his eyes straining. "Patrizia!"

"She's with me," the marine grinned, "you've got yourself a common lass." The words were barely out of his mouth when a fist pummelled his face. Mark swung at him blindly.

The marine attempted to defend himself but alcohol muted his senses. Within a couple of blows, he fell to the floor.

Mark knelt down and continued to pummel him.

"Stop! You'll kill him!"

Patrizia's voice arrested him.

"Where are you, my heart?" He reached out a bloody fist and she grasped it.

At her touch, he began to sob. "I thought I'd lost you."

She made no response and he felt her. "Are you hurt? Did he touch you?"

"No," she whispered, "just a slap."

Mark screamed in anger and kicked the marine's body.

The man groaned, then fell silent.

"Please, no more." Patrizia whispered. Her breath was laboured and Theresa rushed to her.

"We've gotta go, she needs help." Theresa pulled Mark's arm. "Hurry, she could be bleeding."

He turned away abruptly and swung Patrizia into his arms.

"Are you in pain? I'll take you home." He kissed her on the forehead as he walked to the stairs. The leather case lay open in the dirt, its bottles smashed. An overpowering aroma of ointments filled the air.

The marine lifted himself from the floor and groaned as he felt his bruised body.

Mark paused on the landing and called out. "Run, you bastard. If I see you again, you're a dead man."

They walked out into the dusk. The call of kookaburras sounded in the bush as Mark turned towards the point. "You're safe."

Patrizia nodded, her breath erratic.

Theresa noticed that she rubbed her side as Mark strode along.

Images played to her from a tunnel.

The militia man regained consciousness. He staggered from the cellar as whistles sounded in the air. He turned towards the scrub, leaving a bloody trail in his wake.

Dogs barked at the scent, the trail leading to the death bush beyond.

In the cottage, Mark's eyes turned from Kathleen's to the surgeon's.

The surgeon shook his head. "I'll leave her to Kathleen's care. She's the best person now." He patted Mark's arm as he gathered his cape.

Mary spoke in a low voice to Mark as they watched Patrizia lying in bed.

Birth pangs were evident on her white face as she clutched her side and moaned.

Theresa screamed. "Help her, she's bleeding!"

Kathleen's face was non committal as she felt Patrizia's abdomen.

Mark knelt beside the bed, holding a swath of cotton in his arms. A tuft of dark hair was discernible from the cloth and he held it close to Patrizia.

She smiled and stroked the baby's head. "She looks like you."

"Poor child, I'd hoped better for her." He saw her wince as she rubbed her side. Mark threw a pleading glance at Kathleen.

She shook her head and turned away.

Mark held a genesis seed to Patrizia's lips, she swallowed it and smiled at him.

"You're all grace to me," she whispered, "you always were."

"Rest now," he smoothed her hair from her forehead. "Rest, my heart."

The tunnel contracted as Theresa waited for the silence to come. The attic was still in the evening light as she stared out the window.

"Tess, dinner's ready."

"Coming."

Gulls whirled past in the sky, like irritable children.

Ruan's face was clear in her mind as his words echoed in her heart. She too knew the scent of death.

Chapter 28

Sunday sounds everywhere. Wooden boats spilled into the harbour as sails caught wind in exhilarated freedom.

Grace sipped a cup of tea at the window seat as she looked out at the vivid seascape.

"That was Dad on the phone."

Grace looked up to see Theresa approach, smiling. "And?"

"I can visit him next weekend, Sarah's staying with her parents at the Dandenong's. He's booked my ticket."

"Do you want to go?"

Theresa sat on the kitchen bench, shoulders hunched. "Yeah, I wanna see Dad. Maybe I'll call Nick, see if the gang can catch up." She strummed her fingers. "I dunno why Dad squeezes me in when she's away, like he's embarrassed by me."

"Not true. I think Sarah has him on very tight strings. Some people need to compartmentalize their lives, slot people into different times or else it seems all out of control. I did that for years with Stephan, we were our own worst enemies, always controlling each other."

"Do you do it now?"

"Hopefully not as much, not in Sydney anyway. I can't control things as well here, I'm out of my territory."

"Like when I refused to go to Loreto?"

Grace laughed. "Absolutely. It was a good choice, Tess, I can see you're happy. How's Alicia?"

"Good, I'm seeing her next Thursday, we're goin' to the movies with Ruan."

"Is she out of the clinic?"

"No way, but she's allowed to go out for a couple of hours."

"Poor kid, it must be hard for her. We didn't have those issues when

I was a kid, never even thought of starving ourselves. You don't ever feel like that, do you, babes?"

"As if. You've raised me to eat like a pig."

"Thank you, I think."

Theresa looked away as she spoke. "Mum."

"Yes?"

"Do you ever wanna have a boyfriend?"

Grace didn't reply.

"Well?"

"Tough question."

"No it isn't, yes or no."

"Well maybe for you it's black and white but not for me. Sometimes I feel I'm ready and I'd love to. Most of the time I worry about the effect on you and my parents. They're so old fashioned, 'specially Mum. She thinks I should live for you and die alone, a saintly old lady."

"That's so mean!"

"It isn't, it's her generation, eternal love and all that crap. She always thinks your dad will come back to me."

"No chance of that."

"Thank you."

They grinned at each other.

"Y'know, Mum, if you wanted to, I wouldn't mind."

"Thanks. How do you feel about seeing Nick, bit nervous?"

"Yeah but maybe he doesn't want to see me. I'd like to see him, see how I feel when I'm with him. Y'now how everything feels different when you have a boyfriend? Not that he's my boyfriend anymore but I don't know if I'm the same."

"Yes, you change and you can't go back to what you were. I

won't be the same when we go home."

Theresa followed the movement of yachts on the harbour with restless eyes.

Grace's voice called her back. "Do you miss him?"

"I dunno, I think about him a lot, argue with him in my head. Sometimes I miss the stuff we used to do together, I wonder if he does too or if he likes someone else." She grinned. "I should call him now, see if he's free next weekend."

Grace nodded as she sipped her tea.

Theresa dialled the number quickly.

"Hello."

"Hi Mrs Vasoulos. It's Tess."

"Long time no hear. How are your studies going? Nick's got so much on."

"Same with me but it's all good. Is Nick awake?"

"I'm not sure, he might have gone out."

"He usually sleeps in on a Sunday. Can you wake him, I've got something important to tell him."

Pause.

"Sure honey."

Theresa waited, bewildered by the authoritative sound of her own voice.

"Hey."

"Hi Nick. Guess what?"

"You're coming home."

"Yeah. Not forever, just for next weekend."

"Cool, you staying with your dad?"

"Yeah. I wondered if you want to meet on Saturday night with the gang."

"Yeah ok, I'll tell them. Even if they can't come, we can go out."

Pause. "If you want to." Theresa drew in her breath. "Yeah. I'll call you on Saturday and you can let me know where to meet you."

"Cool. Missed ya."

"How much?"

"Wing span of an ostrich."

She laughed. "I'd better go, mum and I do are doing our tourist thing today. We're goin' to Bondi markets."

"Lucky you, I'm going to the Vic markets with Dad to buy fruit and veg."

"Call you Saturday. Bye."

"Bye."

She stood and looked at the attic latch, restless. Abruptly, she moved across to the piano and played a tune. The gentle chords of her other language calmed her.

The remainder of the week an impatient blur.

Ruan looked at her quizzically in class. "What time do we meet Alicia tomorrow?"

"At three o'clock, outside of Hoyts. She'll meet us on the steps."

He twirled a strand of her hair. "Why the look of bliss all week? Have you missed your dad heaps?"

"A bit, not heaps." She looked away. " I'll see Nick on Saturday. We talked and I think he's changing, he's..."

"Whoa, girl. Go slow."

"No really, I think he is."

The blur continued the next day as she walked towards the cinema. George Street felt clean and new to her. She spotted Alicia and Ruan on the cinema steps, Alicia's arms flung outwards in an animated gesture.

"Hey, girl."

"Tess! Ruan just told me the boy wants you back. Make it hard, make him beg." Alicia's cheekbones had filled out slightly and the hollows under her eyes were less sharp.

"I will. You look good." She sat beside them. "What're we seeing?"

"Some crappy thriller Ruan wants to see."

"Violent, full of guns kinda stuff?"

Ruan nodded. "The best, you'll love it. C'mon, let's get our tickets." He led the way to the box office.

The dreamy motion of moving frames swept the audience into intimacy.

Alicia yawned and whispered to Ruan throughout the film.

"That was total shit," she announced as she threw her ticket in the bin at the end of the film. "I can't believe you like that crap."

"We boys are simpletons, y'know that. I owe you coffee for sitting through it."

"You owe us coffee. Tess sat through it, even if she didn't watch it."

Theresa flushed and Alicia nudged Ruan.

"She's in love, what're you gonna do about it?"

"Nothing. C'mon girls, let's go."

They walked outside and flagged a bus down to the Rocks.

Chapter 29

"What time do you have'ta be back?"

"About six thirty, it's the latest they'll serve dinner." Alicia pressed her hands against a shopfront window. "When I was a kid, I used to think the Rocks had an old fashioned smell, y'know like baked bread."

"I used to think I'd see a pirate walk off a ship and start a sword fight with someone," Ruan grinned. "I'm big now, I know pirates only live on islands with mermaids and Peter Pan."

They laughed.

"Let's go to Maxim's Bakehouse, they make the best cappuccinos."

"My neighbour, Peter, loves that place. Must be a guy thing."

Theresa jerked to a stop as she stared at the antiquated signage above her. Her heart seemed to catch in her chest.

"What's up, Tess? you feel OK? Shit, you're not about to have a heart attack are you? I don't know CPR."

Alicia frowned. "She looks like she's seen a ghost."

Theresa stood motionless, her eyes transfixed.

Ruan stood on tiptoe and made the sign swing in the breeze. "Royal Tea Merchant To His Majesty The King, 1792." He read aloud.

The worn red and green letters seemed to sigh at his touch.

"Don't touch it!" Theresa whispered, her face milk white. "Come with me."

She walked to the end of the shop front and looked down the cobblestone pathway that bordered the side.

"It's private property, you can't go down there."

"Do you think she's on drugs?" Alicia peered down. "Maybe she's not as straight as I thought."

Theresa's heart caught in a memory.

She walked on blindly and stopped at a wooden gate, then reached up and unlatched it.

"Whoa, we're in trespass country. Wake up and smell the police charges." Alicia's eyes widened. "This's someone's back garden, we can't go in."

"You have'ta help me, I need to find something."

Ruan spoke gently. "You've lost something?"

"No, I need to find it. Please come."

"OK, princess."

They entered a small garden. Terracotta pots lay strewn across an overgrown lawn, autumn flowers thriving in the cheerful disarray. Theresa crept to the back wall, her hands pressed to the sandstone. On the far side of the building, a low door was locked and signposted.

Ruan read aloud. "Archaeological site, property of the Historical Society of NSW. Unsafe conditions."

Theresa knelt down and pressed her face to the door.

"How'd she know it was there?" Alicia whispered and he shook his head.

"Sh, it means a lot to her." He crouched down. "Tess, what's inside?"

"Something I need."

"It's a heavy duty lock, we can't break this open."

Alicia pushed Ruan aside. "I can." She opened her velvet bag, drew out a nail file and a pair of nail scissors.

"I knew boyfriend number three would come in handy some day," she grinned, "he did time for breaking and entering. I learnt a lot from him." She looked backwards. "Close the gate, Ruan, we don't want any more visitors."

Alicia gently twisted her nail file inside the lock, then flipped the point of the scissors into an upper groove. A smooth click in response. "Done."

Theresa squeezed her arm. "Thanks."

Alicia disconnected the padlock and pushed open the cellar door. She backed away swiftly, holding her nose as a dank smell arose. "Whoa, too rich for me. Chanel no 5 it ain't."

Ruan peered inside the small entrance. "Must've been a colony of midgets two hundred years ago. Bloody dark down there."

"Look," Theresa stepped over him, "they've left a torch hanging on the wall."

"Probably check up on the place from time to time." Ruan switched it on and a powerful beam emanated.

Alicia crouched over them. "Cool, it's like going back in time. Betcha a pirate once drank rum down there."

"Har, har me hearty, right you are."

"Let's go down." Theresa's eyes gleamed.

"No way, Princess, didn't you read the sign? Unsafe conditions, these stairs are probably over two hundred years old. They're not gonna hold all our weight."

"It'd hold mine though."

"It's too risky."

Alicia grabbed the torch. "What're you looking for, Tess? The archeologists would've searched the place and taken anything that was left behind."

"Maybe it's like Pompei, maybe they left artefacts behind."

"I'll go down, I weigh less than both of you. Being anorexic has some advantages."

She tapped the first step and a hollow sound echoed. "Very encouraging. What am I looking for?"

"A black leather case."

"What's in it? diamonds?"

"Herbs."

"I could die for a bunch of herbs? Talk it up at my funeral please."

Alicia tapped the second stair as she descended gingerly.

Ruan made the sign of the cross and Theresa copied him. "I'm turning into my mum." she murmured.

"She's hot."

"You're kidding!"

Below them, a creak sounded and Alicia stood closer to the earthen wall. "It's better here, less worn away." She flashed the torch, revealing flattened soil.

They watched in silence as she neared the end of the stairs. She stumbled on the last step and screamed.

A thud echoed, then blackness entombed the cellar.

Silence.

"Alicia!" screamed Theresa. "Oh God, what's happened? Alicia!"

The torch switched on and Alicia grinned up at them. "Only kidding, didn't you ever see Roman Holiday? Y'know the scene with Gregory Peck and Audrey Hepburn, when he sticks his hand in the wall and starts scream....."

"Shut up! You scared the shit out of me." Theresa breathed heavily. "Sorry, Alicia."

"So you should be, it's no party down here." Alicia shone the torch over the ground.

"Nothin' here, I'll try the walls."

Long beams projected upwards.

"Sorry, no go."

"You'd better come up now, princess. Go slow."

Alicia flashed the torch light behind the stairs and two grey rats ran out and encircled her in a looping dance. They slid into small vents along the ground and Alicia jumped in shock.

"Shit!" she screamed, "oh shit."

She ran to the stairs and climbed them two at a time. The stairs wavered as she pounded the fragile nails with her tred. She pushed past Theresa and Ruan and shook herself on the grass.

"Is there anything on me? Anything having a nibble?"

Ruan held her shoulders. "Keep still, you're OK. Stop yelling or I'll have'ta slap you."

"Just try, dork." She let out a whoop. "That was wicked! Where next Tess, any other cellars near by?"

Theresa looked down at the cellar, her eyes glistening.

"You were brilliant. We'd better go, we won't have time for cappuccinos now, you have'ta get back to Neutral Bay. I'll padlock the doors."

"I'm sorry we didn't find it. What did you want it for anyway?"

"Just something I saw once." Theresa shrugged her shoulders. "You must think I'm mad."

"No, you show real promise as a potential deviant. Top that, Ruan."

"Couldn't. C'mon, we'd better move it, you have'ta go."

They walked down the laneway and Alicia stopped on the street.

"Sure, I'll head off. See ya next week, deviants. Have fun in Melbourne, Tess." She hugged them, then moved into the crowds on George Street.

"I'll walk with you to Martin Place" Ruan called out and he turned to Theresa. "Be safe in Melbourne, make sure your angel looks after you."

"Thanks, see you."

The sandstone streets seemed to reflect her sombre mood as she walked home. Theresa entered the hallway of the terrace and saw a middle aged woman leave Maruska's flat.

"Bye, Madame. Thanks."

"Goodbye, Clara. Make time to practise."

The woman smiled at Theresa as she passed by.

Maruska called out. "Theresa, come and join me for a cup of tea. I'm truly parched."

"Ok thanks. I can't stay long though, I've gotta pack. I'm staying with my Dad this weekend." She looked back as the front door closed. "She's a bit old to be learning piano."

Maruska laughed. "I'm glad you said that after she closed the door. And what's the cut off time for learning? Thirty five? Forty five?"

"I dunno. When brain cells stop regenerating."

"Said with the confidence of youth. Clara's one of my best paying students, she's a merchant banker and very successful. Nothing like a regular cheque to cheer one up and fill the cookie jar."

As Maruska filled the kettle, Theresa stared at a vase of dried lavender on the table. It evoked memories of Patrizia and her eyes filled.

"Do you visit the attic still?"

Theresa's eyes spilled over.

Maruska walked across and hugged her. "Cherub, it's alright to feel grief, it's the price we pay for love. All will be well."

Theresa wiped her eyes. "Have you ever seen it? The cellar?"

"Is it still boarded up?"

"It's padlocked now, my friends helped me open it. I didn't see anything though."

"Just the whisper of love in the quiet earth."

Maruska placed a teacup in front of Theresa. "I looked too as a young girl and was bitterly disappointed. But with time, I was grateful I saw something of Patrizia's life. She was my great, great, great grandmother you know."

Theresa stared as she continued on. "Didn't I tell you? This house has been in my family for many generations."

Theresa sipped her tea.

"Did you ever find the genesis seed? Does it still exist?"

"My cherub, it's everywhere. Everyone has access to the seed."

"I didn't know, I though it's secret died with Patrizia."

"Would you like one? Just a minute." Maruska walked across to the Kookaburra stove and reached up to the shelf above it. She took a pottery jar down and pulled the cork top free, then shook a seed into her hand.

"Try one, they're quite tangy."

Theresa's hand trembled, the aroma of the homeopathic cottage in England whispered on her skin. She chewed it and her nose wrinkled.

"It's bitter."

"An acquired taste, I agree. Would you like to take some with you?"

"Yes, please."

Maruska shook a handful into a small glass jar. "The desire for love's strong. I've needed the genesis seed in my life too."

"Did it help you?"

"It gave me a true answer, no more, no less."

The buzzer sounded and she stood. "My next pupil. Good luck, Theresa. I hope your answer's the one you seek." She hugged her.

"Thanks Maruska. I...." Theresa tried to speak. "Thanks" she whispered.

She walked upstairs, the jar held tight in both hands.

Chapter 30

Theresa remembered her childhood dream that she could fly. She shook her head at the air hostess offering drinks. Clouds blurred the view to a ghostly landscape. The Captain announced arrival in ten minutes and Theresa felt anxious at seeing her dad and Nick. Familiar strangers.

The terminal was abuzz with tourists in the city of trams as her father embraced her at the arrivals gate.

"Tess, it's good to hug you again! You've lost weight, been studying too hard?" He picked up her bag and they walked to the carpark. Theresa glanced at him, he looked older, his hair completely grey now.

She clutched her cardigan. "Ugh, it's colder here than in Sydney. How's Sarah, does she look fat?"

"Don't let her hear you say that! Women are so neurotic about their weight, you're supposed to gain weight when you're pregnant. I don't get all the angst."

"Poor dad. Have you got lots of baby stuff yet? Mum says you should start practising sleep deprivation now, so it's not so hard when the baby comes."

"Did she? What are her ideas?"

"Oh y'know, sleep for four hours, then stay up for twenty. She said sometimes I did that to her."

"I don't remember that."

"Well it was a long time ago, Dad. I'm nearly eighteen."

"Unbelievable! Will you be in Melbourne for your birthday?"

"I dunno, Mum hasn't said anything. I've got some way cool friends at Tafe, I might go clubbing with them to celebrate."

"Watch out for blokes trying to spike your drink, I hear that happens a lot in Sydney."

"Dad!"

"Sorry, Tess, I can't help with the advice. How's Tafe, is it as good as your old school?"

"Settle Dad, it's all cool. You get a lot more independence at Tafe, Mum says it's just like uni."

"Without all the creeps, I hope. Do you have any Italian friends?"

"Nup, I know a really nice Spanish guy though. His dad's got a restaurant in the Spanish quarter in town."

"Keep away from that lot. Once in the restaurant game, always in it." Theresa rolled her eyes.

"I'm not marrying the guy, we're just friends. But I have a so cool girlfriend, Alicia. She wants to be a fashion designer."

"Good luck to her, there's lots of money in fashion nowadays."

"Yeah, I guess. She has to get over her anorexia first. You'd love her, Dad. She's a Gothic and really smart."

They walked on in silence before her dad spoke again. "Must be some troubled kid. Don't you start imitating her."

"Dad, I have my own mind. You don't have'ta say stuff I already know."

"Sorry, Tess. I don't see you on a regular basis, it's a lot to take on in one go. Your mum hears it all the time, it's not such a shock for her. Anyway, I'm a financial planner, I always tell everyone what to do."

He looked ahead. "How's Grace? Does she like her job, like Sydney?"

"She's brilliant, we get on heaps better now. Mum's much less anal, she says it's because she's out of her territory."

"Is she seeing anyone?"

"She hasn't told me. We've got a mad neighbour downstairs, Peter.

He's an artist, I think he likes Mum a bit."

"What about her?"

"She wouldn't tell me, I'm the last one to know anything. I don't mind if she finds a boyfriend, she's been on her own a long time."

"If she finds one in Sydney, she won't want to move back soon."

"Whatever." Theresa grinned. "Mum started bellydancing this winter, said she wanted to be in touch with her inner showgirl."

"Typical Grace. Start something knowing she'll never carry it through. She's always doing that."

"Like when?"

"Well, she took up a Thai cooking course, lasted four classes."

"She said it was boring."

"Well I thought it was really practical, something she could have for life."

Theresa was silent until they reached the car park. "Dad."

"Yes?"

"Do you ever take time off? Do stuff?"

"You must be kidding, I've no time. We've just finished the extension at the back of the house, the baby's due in a couple of months and Sarah's family are always inviting us to stay over or they come to us. Work's really busy and my bloody clients can't make a decision without phoning me a hundred times. I don't have time to scratch myself."

She squeezed his arm. "I'll look after you. Let's look around the city, go for a cappuccino on Lygon street."

He unlocked the boot of the car. "Parking in the city's hideously expensive, let's go home. Sarah's bought an espresso machine."

He opened the passenger door. "Is Grace going out much?"

"Yeah, we play tourist on the weekends. We go out for dinner on Sunday nights."

"Every Sunday?"

"Yeah."

"Knew it."

"What?"

"Never mind." He smiled. "Enough about your mum. C'mon, let's head home. I think you'll really like the back patio."

Theresa stared out the window as they reached suburbia. Trams passed by, like mechanical prima donnas. Couples power walked through parks, with trees blown bare by autumnal winds. Well dressed old ladies waited at bus stops, dressed for high tea at the Windsor Hotel.

The inner city suburbs appeared more cloistered to her.

"We're here."

She stepped outside to the scent of mown lawns. "You've been painting."

"Yes, finished last weekend. Sarah wanted the toxins to subside before baby arrives."

"Where's the nursery?"

Stephan opened the front door and pointed. "The old study, we converted it."

She ran over. "Oh Dad!"

She looked at the cot and vivid animal friezes on the walls. The curtains were draped.

"Sarah did a great job." She stroked the giraffe toy in the cot. "It's brilliant."

"I thought you'd like it. We're so excited. Sarah will be a great mum, she's wanted a child for a long time."

"I know. Mum says the baby year is the most tiring but best year you'll ever have. She loved the smell of me as a baby, said I was all milky and gooey."

"I don't remember that, I was working crazy hours. This time I'll cut back, give Sarah more of a hand than I did your mum." He held out his arm. "Come have a look at the patio."

"If I have to."

He pointed to some seedlings stacked in a corner. "I'm planting these out here. When I've done that, it'll look finished. Hopefully they'll be in by the end of the weekend. It'll be easier with Sarah away."

"Oh. Do you mind if I call Nick?"

"How come you're calling him? I thought it was off."

"It is, we're just gonna meet up with the gang from school tonight. I haven't seen them in ages."

"Ok, don't be long on the phone."

She headed inside and dialled the number.

"Hey Tess, what time did you get here?"

"Bout an hour ago. It feels weird being back, like I'm home but I'm not."

"How long you here?"

"Till Sunday night, I've got Tafe on Monday. I was up till one this morning studying so I could take the weekend off. Have you got heaps of stuff to do?"

"Yeah but I haven't finished any. I'll have'ta do most of it this weekend."

She was silent as he continued on. "But we're still OK to go out tonight, Tom and Despina are coming, everyone else is studying."

"Where'll we meet?"

"Chinatown, six o'clock in front of the Chinese dragons. We'll go to the movies after dinner."

"It'll be good to see you all. Bye Nick."

"Yeah..."

She hung up quickly and walked out to the patio.

"Want to help, Tess? I've got a spare pair of gloves. We haven't gardened together in ages."

"Years dad, let's keep it that way." She sat on the patio table and swung her legs.

Her heart felt light, like an angel sat on her shoulder protecting her.

Chapter 31

Grace clipped her hair up as she went to answer the knock at her front door.

"Peter."

"Melbournite, you finally have the chance to repay me. Aren't you thrilled?"

"What do you mean?"

"I need a favour."

She eyed him suspiciously. "Go on."

"I need to borrow your head."

She laughed.

"Pardon?"

"Actually, your profile to be exact. Turn to the side."

She did so automatically and he reached across and stroked her cheek.

"It's perfect. You're home today?"

"Depends what you want my head for."

"I need to sketch you."

"No bloody way." She backed away from the door. "I'm working from home this weekend, Tess is at her Dad's. And I've got stacks of ironing to catch up on. Currently, all I have ironed are my pyjamas."

"You iron your pyjamas?"

"Yes and my sheets and tea towels. Ask my girl, I have no life and I never pretended to."

"Don't get so defensive, Melbournite. Just think, this is your chance to be immortalised on canvas. People will admire the wanton abandon of your silhouette. Your friends may see it hanging in a gallery in Melbourne and gossip about how Grace became an artist's model. Please, I need your help. One hour, tops."

"Don't do this to me, I'm the wrong person to ask."

"I won't keep you long. Just let me show you what I need."
She hesitated and he held his hand out.
"Please, Grace."
"It won't work, I'll tell you now."
He watched, bemused, as she collected her keys and locked her door.
"Why are you locking up? I'm not asking you to move in with me."

She flushed. "Very funny. I come from a security conscious family, we locked everything. Ten times a day. Twelve if we were really conscientious."
"You have an endearing eccentricity about you. It's at odds with your corporate image."
"If I decide to stay, you've got me for half an hour."
Peter nodded and led the way to his flat. He motioned to the easel in the middle of the room. "My problem."
Grace walked across and studied it. A beach scene was sketched in pencil on the canvas and attached to the right hand corner was a photograph of a woman.

"But you got someone already."
"She's not right for the scene. I knew I should have asked a brunette to pose on the rock."
"You asked a stranger to pose for your camera?"
"Of course. Women are flattered when you tell them you want to paint them. A little wax lyrical is in every artist's repertoire." He leaned closer. "Don't tell me you haven't learned the art of bullshitting in the corporate world. It must be part of your salary package."
"It is," she sighed. "Well, where's your camera? I can't take my hair out, I haven't washed it in four days."
"I'll sketch you first."
"But you only took that woman's photo."

"Of course, she was a stranger. You're a dear friend. It's not often I have a live model to sketch. Women don't accept my propositions like they used to. No, no you're here and I'm going to keep you. Don't suppose you'd get your kit off?"

"Very funny. Only if you get yours off."

"Done."

She started and moved towards the door.

"I'm only kidding, Melbournite. Now, I need you to sit on the floor over there, on top of the towels. Turn to your side and gather your legs with your left arm and stare in the distance."

"That's tricky, since I'm facing a wall half a metre from me."

"Use your imagination!"

"How long will this take?"

"Are we there yet?" He motioned to the towels and she moved across and sat down.

"I feel so silly," she murmured as he knelt in front of her.

He tilted her profile downwards and unclipped her hair. It cascaded down and he arranged it over her shoulders.

"Move your left arm, Grace. No, not so stiffly, loosen that pose a bit. Softer, that's it."

She blinked.

"Don't fiddle. It's unbecoming to a sexy woman like you."

"When you're finished, I'll strangle you."

"Such threats of violence."

"Shut up! I feel stupid enough and you keep tormenting me with smarmy comments. If you want a favour from me, can't you at least be pleasant and not make me feel uncomfortable the whole time?"

She half stood.

"Please don't go. I'll behave, I promise."

She sat and repositioned herself.

"Thank you."

He was silent as he commenced sketching, the scrap of his pencil rhythmic in the still room.

Grace tried to sit still.

"I appreciate your making time for me, I really do. Flippant is what I do best, we've all got our defence mechanisms, you know that."

She stayed silent.

"Don't suppose you could soften your expression a little? Your eyes could burn a hole in that wall. I'm trying to capture a reflective mood, not Hannibal Lector at the beach."

She laughed.

'Now I know what you mean about your temper."

"You provoked me, Peter. You know you did."

"It's entirely my fault. Now will you strip for me?"

"No chance. Anyway, I look better fully clothed. Anyone over forty does."

"Speak for yourself. I'm an Adonis in the buff."

"Of course. Are you nearly done?"

"No, be patient. Soften that gaze, Grace, think of something that makes you go all marshmallowy."

"I'm struggling."

He turned to the canvas and Grace listened to the sounds of his craft.

Outside, a seagull cawed.

"Lovely," Peter murmured, "you've caught the emotion of the scene. Not everyone does.

"I thought you concentrated on landscapes."

"I was waiting for you to ask about that." He crouched down beside her and kissed the top of her head.

"Thank you. Come and see."

The top of her head tingled where his lips had brushed her.

"What do you think?"

For the first time, Grace saw a trace of anxiety in his eyes as she walked across to the easel. He had sketched her sitting on a rock. A wash of sea struck the rock, causing her to turn and watch the motion. A cliff face behind her was dominated by a telecommunications tower.

"Well?"

"I look fat."

"Every woman's lament."

"Couldn't you change that bit? Take a few centimetres off my waist."

"No," he moved her hand away gently, "I love the female body, the soft curves. So Rubensque."

"Bastard."

"Is that your opinion of my sketch?"

He looked hurt.

"No, it's just a bit startling to see myself like that. I'm sure it will be an amazing painting. I'm glad you picked my curves to squat on the rock."

"Are you making up to me, Grace?"

"Yes."

They laughed and Peter motioned to the drinks cabinet.

"Why not? Scotch please."

"This could turn into a regular date."

"About the closest I've come in the last ten years."

"So long? I'd go insane without the physical contact. No relationships at all?"

"Just Tess."

"Well, she's great."

"Thank you."

"I didn't know anyone could grow up that virtuous in Australia."
"Just add the migrant experience and shake well. Viola! Instant virtue."
"The protective dad?"
"A shotgun for every occasion."
He handed her the drink and they moved across to the sofa. Peter flicked on the CD player and Grace curled up as she listened to the music.
"You like old gravel throat?"
"Mr Dylan? Yeah, always have. That yearning for a simpler time resonates with me."

"We're two sides of a coin, Grace. I've been promiscuous and you've been the opposite. But we've both needed...." he smiled. "I don't know what."
"So why are you adding people to your landscapes?"
"I don't know." His eyes squinted as late afternoon light flooded the room. "As an artist, you change and you can't explain why. I'm craving people in my landscapes, not full on portraiture. Profiles and silhouettes in an imperfect landscape."

He grinned. "You ever suddenly change and can't explain why?"
"Yes."
"Go on."
She laughed and sipped her drink.
"I'm different in Sydney. In Melbourne, I have perfect control of my life. I'm ahead on my mortgage, I pay my credit card off monthly, my fruit and veg man knows me by name. Here, I'm lost. My tenants are behind one month in their rent and there's nothing I can do about it. My dad's having a hip operation next month and I can't get time

off to be there for him. I pay double for everything and I miss my girlfriends. I should hate the chaos but I don't. I love it. It's like your half finished painting, I don't know how it will turn out or if I'll like it and I don't care."

She bent her head. "That was a really long answer. Sorry."
"You open up with a glass of spirits."
"Keep drinking, I want to hear your secrets."
"None to tell."
"There's one," she grinned, "you said last time I was here, that in the end there was no one to go home to in the country. Who was there initially?"
"Sally."
"More please. After my soliloquy, I deserve details."
He leaned back and closed his eyes.
Grace nudged him with her foot.
"I can't hear you."

"Sally McIntosh. She lived on the next property and she made my childhood bearable. My father thought I was a waste of space, I did art class in town and he was ashamed of my lack of physicality. In the end, I became invisible to him. Sally and I would take off for the day and not come back till night. We'd dig clay from the top paddock and mould shapes, then fire them over an open fire. She was my best mate." He grinned. "I told her we'd never marry but travel the world together. She always smiled."

He looked down. "Then I came to Sydney and she drifted away from me. I didn't see it for ages, wouldn't see it. But, in the end, I became invisible to her too."
He brushed his eyes with his hand. "I haven't talked about her like that in years. Amazing how you can tap into the pain again."

"I know," Grace whispered. "When Stephan told me Sara was pregnant, I was shattered. I knew I would never experience that again. Yet he can do it till his balls freeze over."

"Is he planning to have them frozen?"

"It'd be a fitting end." She drained her glass. "Thanks, this was unexpectedly fun."

"Thank you, muse. I'll invite you to the exhibition my gallery's planning."

"Great," she stood and moved to the door. "How do they market you?"

"Neurotic urban artist obsessed with recreating the landscapes of his childhood."

She laughed.

"I appreciate it, Grace." He kissed her lips. "And you don't look fat."

She clung to the balustrade as she walked upstairs. Her phone rang and she ran to answer it.

Chapter 32

"Here's my mobile, Tess. Call me when you're ready." Stephan glanced at her. "You look gorgeous."

"OK, Dad. Thanks."

He ruffled her hair and she pushed him away.

"Stop, you smell of dirt."

"Good, it'll put the boys off."

She blew him a kiss as he drove past.

Theresa pulled her scarf up to cover her neck. Little Bourke Street ran long and narrow in front of her, like a Chinese dragon that sheltered wares underneath its belly.

Elderly Chinese women stood in groups, talked of Maoism, cultural revolutions and the price of rice.

A southerly wind pierced her. Red lanterns hung over doorways as chimes rang in the twilight. Theresa saw the dragons ahead and a dark haired girl waved at her. A boy lounged beside the girl.

"Hey, Tess, over here!" The girl rushed ahead and hugged her. "Too long girl."

"Good to see you, Despina."

"Are you even taller? I'm so a midget next to you."

"Mum reckons I've grown, says it's the harbour air. Hi, Tom."

"Hi."

Despina held her arm. "I can't believe you live in Sydney. What's it like? How's Tafe?"

"The best, I wish I did it last year, they treat you like an adult. Everyone OK at school?"

Tom rolled his eyes. "I can hardly wait to get out, I'm so over school rules."

"Hey."

Theresa turned at the sound of Nick's voice. She hugged him and a silence ensued.

Nick folded his arms. "It's freezin' out here, let's get something to eat."

They followed behind him automatically. He stopped at a restaurant with a damaged neon sign. "It's crap looking but the food's really good."

He walked inside and they followed in procession.

"You look good, Tess."

"You too. Did you get some assignments done?"

"Yeah, kinda. Should we order? I know some really good dishes."

He beckoned a waiter across and ordered. "That OK with everyone?"

"You could order anything, I wouldn't know the difference." Tom laughed.

"Peasant. Hey you two, stop pawing each other."

Theresa raised an eyebrow at Despina.

"It's back on?"

Despina looked between Theresa and Nick, eyebrow raised in return. Theresa looked away.

Nick strummed his fingers on the table. "What's it like being back in town?"

"Different, like I'm home but I'm not. Dad's been gardening all day, so I hung about the house and went shopping to the mall. Kinda boring."

"Girl, shopping's so much more, it's the essence of life."

"Despina, you should meet my friend Alicia, she's awesome. She goes to op shops and retro stores."

"Old stuff, yuk!"

"She looks brilliant in them. We don't wear a uniform, I had to buy heaps of new stuff."

"Lucky you, I'm still wearing the nun's habit. Catholic schools want you to look ugly as. Do you have recess and lunch?"
"Nup, if you have a break between lectures, you can go to the cafes. We usually go for a cappuccino in the morning."
"How come you didn't go to that private school?"
"Didn't feel right, so I refused to go."
"Weren't you scared?"
"No." Theresa felt Despina's eyes were appraising her.
"Nick says you've got a harbour view."
"Yeah but we're at the wrong end of town. We don't look out over gorgeous houses or yacht clubs, just a wharf. Sometimes we see yachts on the weekend, that's pretty cool. But mostly it's cruise ships and container ships."
"Better than seeing my neighbours washing line from my bedroom window." Despina nestled her head on Tom's shoulder. "Are you coming back in December?"

"Suppose so, mum hasn't said anything. I can't believe it's already been six months."
Two adroit waiters approached, dishes balanced on their arms.
"This looks great, Nick. I love red plum duck."
He held the broccoli aloft and Theresa shook her head.
"Never liked broccoli, always felt like I was eating miniature trees."
Tom snorted. "Anything green is offensive, I prefer hamburgers."
"Philistine, next time we'll leave you at McDonalds."
"Suit me fine."
Despina gingerly took a portion of duck. "Poor little thing."

Theresa glanced at Nick, admired the square set of his shoulders as he spoke.
"They should take English off the VSC."

"Why?"

"It's rubbish, no one makes money out of studying poetry."

"I bet J.K. Rowling read poetry as a teenager. She's richer than the Queen now."

"She's a freak." He held Theresa's gaze. "No guys gonna study English at Uni. Only if they fail everything else."

"So it's a girl thing?"

"You said it."

"You implied it."

"What's with the cross examination? You gonna be a lawyer?"

"It wouldn't take me long to knock over your argument if I was."

Despina whistled.

"Go girl. Nick hates to lose an argument."

"Who said I lost it? We haven't even started."

"What's your argument then?"

"It's rude to argue with the guest of honour."

Theresa laughed. "I'm used to arguments, I live with my Mum."

Despina leaned across. "Is she still obsessed about your study and piano practise?"

"I refused to do piano lessons in Sydney. She's OK with it."

Despina eyes widened as Theresa continued on. "She's cooler to live with. I even kind of missed her today."

"Dig up, girl. Are you serious?"

"Yeah."

"What's it like living in the city?"

She looked at Despina thoughtfully as she spoke. "Exciting. Noisy. The drunks stagger past at night and keep us awake."

"Who's the Sydney guy that Nick talks about?"

"Ruan? He's no one special."

"Is he cute in a no one special way?"

Nick leaned forward. "He looks like a horse."

"No he doesn't."

"You told me he did."

"I don't think so now."

"So he looks like a donkey to you now?"

"What's it to you?"

Despina interrupted them. "People, let's chill out. I need to see a photo of this guy."

"I don't have one."

"Well take one and I'll decide what he looks like."

"He just looks like a regular guy."

"Maybe we should talk about poetry again."

They all laughed awkwardly.

Theresa racked her mind for conversation. "Tom, have you decided what you'll do next year?"

"As little as possible."

Nick grinned. "You already do that."

"I might work for a year in my old man's business."

"Do that and you'll never leave. That's what happens."

"How do you know?"

"I've seen it happen before. You'll have one job for life, get married at twenty five, kids at thirty and you're stuck forever."

Despina sat back stiffly as Nick continued.

"It's your life mate." He glanced at his watch. "We've missed the start of the next session at Hoyts. Let's go for a walk instead, maybe for a cappuccino at Southbank."

The night air a sharp embrace as they walked outside. Despina and Tom held hands as they walked ahead.

Theresa hunched forward. "Burr, I forgot how cold it gets."

"Sydney wuss." He held her arm as a tram whizzed past in front of them.

"Am not, you should try catching a bus down George street. Sydney bus drivers are out to maim you, I think they put notches on their belts for how many legs they break a year."

Despina waved from across the street and called out. "We'll meet you across the bridge, at Southbank." They disappeared ahead.

"Do you still hang out with the Spanish guy?"

"Ruan? Oh yeah, we see Alicia together."

"See her? does she go to a special part of Tafe?"

"We all hang out together, as much as we can. You still planning to go to Uni?"

"Yeah, millionaire by thirty, retired at forty, living on an island at fifty."

"Better than living here." She shivered as they crossed Swanston Street Bridge. The brown hue of the Yarra River was psychedelically distorted by city lights.

She stopped abruptly and rested her hands on the bridge rails. From her bag, she shook a seed out of the jar and held it out.

"Like one?" her hand trembled, "they're pretty spicy."

"What's this? You doin' drugs in Sydney?"

Theresa looked at his lips, the first lips she ever kissed.

"It's just a seed, it's natural, will you try it? It's good for you, it brings you..." Her voice extinguished under his curious eyes.

He rolled the seed on his palm. "What's it do?"

"Trust me."

"I don't do anything unless I know what the outcome is."

A wind rose from the river and Nick put his hands in his jacket.

"C'mon, let's join them. When we're in the café, I'll look at it, see if I can work out what it is."

"I don't think so, you're not meant to understand it. Let's go, it's freezing out here."

As she spoke, she sealed the lid of the jar, then tossed it down to the river below.

They walked in silence along the bridge.

A tiny splash sounded below them. It was lost in the sound of the wind and traffic.

Chapter 33

Theresa stared out the plane window, enchanted by the harbour city at night. It was like a glimpse into the mind of a supernatural artist. City towers glittered like fluorescent chess pieces, ready to be reassembled by a giant's hand.

She felt on edge, her emotions heightened inexplicably.

Grace waited at the arrivals lounge as passengers disembarked. "Babes, over here!"

Theresa caught her eye and waved.

"Tess, I missed you. The tourist thing wasn't the same without you."

She scanned her mum's face. "What's wrong, Mum? Something's up."

Grace hesitated. "Alicia's sick, she's in St Vincent's Hospital. Ruan called me yesterday." She watched her daughter's face whiten.

"Apparently she took an ecstasy tablet and collapsed. The day you went to the movies, she didn't go back to the clinic."

"I knew," Theresa remembered Alicia's face when they parted.

"Mum, I knew she'd do something but I didn't say anything."

"You might have suspected something was up but you couldn't have known what she'd do. Let's go home, you can see her tomorrow morning. I'll come with you, I'll call work from the hospital, tell them I'll be late."

"No, I want to go tonight. Please, Mum, let's go."

"Babe, she's in a coma, critical but stable. Ruan will be there in the morning, there's nothing you can do now."

Theresa silently cajoled her with her eyes.

"Ok, honey, we'll go."

They sat in silence as Grace pulled into the city expressway and took the turn off to Taylor Square. She negotiated the traffic congestion and finally pulled into the hospital car park.

The car park lift took them to a carpeted vision of clinical order. "This way."

Grace turned into a side corridor. Half open doors allowed glimpses of tubed limbs under rumpled white sheets. A voyeuristic vision of frailty. Nurses walked about, silent sentinels. Grace stopped outside a heavy plastic door, which reflected a blurred row of beds. Each bed was hooked to a flashing machine.

"Ready?"

Theresa nodded.

A middle aged couple looked up as they entered the room.

"How is she, Margaret, any change?"

"Mildly deteriorated when they changed her tubes, she stirred but didn't open her eyes."

She glanced across. "You must be Theresa, you look just like your mum."

Theresa stared in disbelief.

Grace held Margaret's hand. "Why don't you both come for a cup of tea with me? Tess's here, she'll stay with Alicia while you have a break. I'll let the intensive care nurse know we're going downstairs." Grace gently guided them through the doors. "Is Ruan still here? he'll want to come up now."

A whispered reply, then silence.

Theresa stood near the doorway as the intensive care nurse scanned charts attached to the end of beds. Lives summarized by a brief synopsis.

Theresa approached Alicia's bed. A tube was pressed into her arm, Theresa could see the sticky fluid enter her veins, felt it enter her bloodstream.

Alicia's face was obscured by a mask, her black hair fanned

outwards on the pillow case.

Theresa waited, yet all remained as it was. The curtains were drawn back, Taylor Square lights looked an impressionistic blur in the distance.

"Hey, princess."

Theresa started.

Ruan stood inside the doorway. "You just got back?"

"Yeah, Mum drove me. She must've been here today."

"Yeah, and yesterday. Grace let me know how Alicia was, I stayed downstairs at reception."

He looked at Alicia's bed, his eyes unreadable. "I hate this smell."

"I can't smell a thing."

"You have'ta be born with it, like a dog hears a silent whistle."

"When's she gonna wake up? Do they know?"

"They don't know if she will. She's been sick a long time."

"But she said she went to the anorexia clinic for the first time only two years ago."

"She's had anorexia since she was little, her parents told me. The specialist said that her organs are weak from all the years of starvation. The ecstasy tablet was low grade but it stopped her heart beating. The ambulance revived her at the club but she went into a coma." He backed away. "Let's go outside, we can talk in the lounge area."

Theresa held his arm. "I can't leave her, I promised Mum I'd stay."

"Tess, I can't stay."

"Please don't leave me."

He gently shook his arm free and moved across to the window.

Theresa stood alongside Alicia and gathered her hair softly. A machine whirred as she bent over and kissed her. "Hey, princess, I'm here. Keep strong girl." She made the sign of the cross and whispered a prayer.

Ruan bent his head and wept silently.

The muffled sound caught her ear and she approached him. "It's OK, you love her too."

He tried to straighten but Theresa held him close.

"Ruan, it's alright to cry."

His face turned away, he held out a fist to Theresa. "Put this in her hands."

"No, you do it. I'll come with you," she led him across. "Here's her hand, you can touch, it won't hurt her."

He trusted her directions like a child and pressed Alicia's hand softly, then backed away.

She smiled as she looked down. "She'd love that."

He moved back to the window and pressed his face against the glass.

Voices sounded in the hallway as Grace entered the room. She stared across at Ruan as

Theresa spoke. "Mum, I'll take Ruan outside and get him some water."

"Good idea."

Alicia's parents stood at the foot of the bed and stared at the silver cross that glittered in Alicia's vacant hand.

The alpha and omega of existence.

A call echoed in Theresa's heart, she smelt the aroma of ghost gums and wattle, knew she had to visit the attic one last time.

The lounge was deserted, littered with paper cups and torn magazines.

Ruan lay on the sofa and held Theresa's hand. His eyelids were swollen and half shut against the fluorescent light. They curled close, Theresa's arm about him.

A murmur within the intensive care unit grew to loud voices and the silence around them splintered into fragments.

Grace ran into the corridor, motioned to a team of people that ran down the corridor towards her, then stood aside as the plastic door flapped shut.

She walked across to them and sat down. "Stay, we can't go in now."

A cry as a machine pummelled Alicia's chest. "Bring her back!"

Grace bent her head, folded her hands in prayer.

Ruan tightened his hold on Theresa's hand and they looked at each other, without words.

The machine stopped and the voices were calmer in the room beyond.

"I'll check on her." Grace ran across and peered in through the plastic door.

"She's dead," Ruan lay back on the sofa. "I know."

"No, she'll make it. I feel it."

"You don't get it, she might survive this time but her body's already damaged. It's a matter of time, Tess." He sighed. "In the end, the sun always lies to you, that beautiful light takes away the people you love."

She pressed his hand and felt his fingers curl around hers. "I believe in Alicia."

"I believe in you."

She flushed.

Grace approached, smiling. "She's held on, I could see from the doorway that they've stabilized her, she's stronger than they give her credit."

"Can we see her, Mum?"

"Just peer in from the doorway, like I did, don't get in anyone's way. Her parents are pretty distraught at the moment."

Theresa held out her hand to Ruan and he took it.

Chapter 34

It was dawn as Theresa looked out at the awakened city. Car headlights flashed across the Harbour Bridge, surreal beacons in the early light.

She stood in the attic and cradled the book. "Will you break my heart again?" She whispered. She sat down, head bowed.

An unfamiliar lullaby sung in a woman's voice. Theresa closed her eyes, soothed by the antiquated melody.

"Don't forget me, Tilly."

Theresa opened her eyes. She stood on a pier close to Patrizia's cottage and she looked about eagerly.

Mary stood alongside her, holding a black haired toddler.

"She won't forget you in a hurry." Mark swung onto the pier from the stern of a boat wharfed alongside it. "I've no words to thank you for all you've done for us."

"And what's that? I've been gifted with this beautiful creature for a year, she's as close to a daughter as I'll ever get. My Ned's so tall, he won't let me hold his hand in the village now." She sighed. "They grow too fast."

Matilda grasped at her cap and Mary laughed. "You've your mother's spirit, she was like a sister to me." Her eyes filled and she looked away as she spoke. "It's a fine day for your move. Will you have help at the other end to unload your furniture?"

"I've organised my convict labourers to meet me at Parramatta wharf. They're good men. They've helped me clear the land this past year. We start on the river frontage next week."

"We'll visit when you're settled. Ned can't wait to see farming land, he's his grandfather's blood in him."

"Send him along now, he can stay with us and experience it first hand. I never thought I'd settle on the land again. If someone had told me twenty years ago where I'd end up, I'd have laughed in their face."

Mary hesitated before she spoke. "Are you sure you'll manage? Tilly's still a baby."

"Governor Grose has given me a housekeeper. Apparently she's first class, an old Irish thief from the First Fleet. I'll have to hide the silver in Tilly's cot."

Mary laughed and held the baby tighter. "I'll miss you both. You're dear to give up your freedom to raise the little one."

"She's already motherless, poor scrap. She'll have a knockabout father do both jobs."

"She's blessed," Mary's voice caught. "I pray she keeps your heart awake."

"I won't find another, if that's what you mean."

"No, I don't. Some men turn savage when they lose their women. Can't love anyone again, including their own. Love Tilly as much as you loved her mother. Patrizia would want that."

Mark held his arms out to Matilda. "Are you ready, bush baby? Let's go."

He hugged Mary tight, then strode towards the boat.

Theresa followed behind as he untied the rope.

Matilda gurgled in his arms as they set off, nestled in Mark's lap as he held the rudder with one hand.

"Look sharp, bush baby."

As he passed the point, he gave one last look at the cottage.

Matilda's face fell as Mary's waving figure became more distant.

"Stop that! you're under new orders now." His face softened.

"Didn't I visit you often enough in this last year? Has a bit of bristle made me unrecognisable?"

He began to sing a lullaby and she stopped mid cry.

"I see, I see, the deep blue sea
  Won't you sail away with me."
She gurgled approvingly.
"You're a regular sailor, bush baby. All you need is a ballad and sea legs. We'll get along just fine."
Theresa stared at the river, grief stricken. The water caught her gaze in hypnotic motion and she closed her eyes and waited for the sensation to pass.

....

She opened her eyes to another cloudless day and all had changed about her. She sat in a ploughed field, the scent of mint and rosemary at her feet.
"Papa, Papa! Look at my potatoes." A child of about ten ran past her and stopped in front of a man standing in the field.
Mark put down his plough and wiped his hands on his clothes. "You didn't see me do that, Tilly. Sarah grumbles that I don't wash my hands at the well, or you for that matter."
"If it's good enough for you, Papa."
"Well it's not good enough for you, currency lass. How'll I raise a well mannered child if she wipes dirt on her clothes and wears long pants?" He grinned. "Did you finish your history lesson?"
"I did. I've learned all the names of the Kings and Queens of England. It was King George who was mean to Mama and sent her away on the big ships."

"He did but look at the blessing I have because of it." He looked up at the sky. "Will you give me another hour before we do my reading lesson?"

"I will but don't forget Mary and Thomas are coming to dinner tonight. Sarah's baking a chicken and I'm to bake the potatoes. Mary said they'll stay the night in the guest house."

"The shed, you mean." Mark said drily. "And that's why I'm getting so fat, Sarah's famous Irish potatoes. Other settlers have offered her double housekeeper wages but she stays with us. You can't buy loyalty, Tilly."

"She says she stays because she can't trust you to raise me proper."

"Oh and an old Irish thief can! Don't tell her I said that, Tilly."

Her eyes twinkled. "What's it worth?"

"No bribes. I can see Sarah's influence already."

They both turned at the sound of the gate latch opening. A young man, of no more than twenty years, pushed the gate. At the sight of them, he hesitated.

His skin declared him a citizen of another country, of snow and soft spring.

Mark moved forward swiftly to greet him. "I knew you'd come one day. I sent so many letters, all unanswered."

"All kept from me. It's good to meet you, Sir."

"And you."

Matilda hung back shyly.

The young man crouched down to her. "I've seen you before."

A high frown appeared on her forehead. "Where?"

"In your mother's face."

"What do you know of my Mama? She's long gone to God."

"Well said. I knew her when I was a little boy, about your age."

"You're not King George's son?"

He laughed. "No."

"Good. If you were, I'd knock you down."

Mark grinned. "We breed them feisty out here."

Jonathon felt inside his pocket. "I've something for you."
Mark quietly walked away as Matilda held out her hand for a small velvet box. She peered inside and was silent.
A ruby ornament glinted in the sunshine and she held it aloft.
Mark returned to them, a small silver urn in his hands.
She ran to him. "Papa, look! It's a funny shaped possum."
"That's not a possum Tilly, it's a squirrel. They live in Europe, where mama came from."
She stared at the ornament, enchanted.
"Do you like it?"
"Very much. Thank you, sir."
"Jonathon, not sir."

She gazed at him thoughtfully. "Did you love my Mama?"
"Very much. She was the happiest memory of my childhood."
"Don't you have a Mama?"
"Yes but she married again after my father died. She gave that ornament to me, she couldn't wear it anymore. I don't see her now. "
"You must be sad."
"No."
Jonathon stood and took the urn from Mark's outstretched hands.
"I've no words to thank you for this, Jonathon. I won't make my way back to England again."
"None are needed, sir. It'll be the honour of my life."
Mark looked away as he spoke. "We're having friends over for dinner tonight. We'd be honoured if you'd stay the night."
"I'd love to." Jonathon crouched beside Matilda. "I've so many stories to tell you about your mother. She was enchanting."
Matilda's eyes were fixed on his face as she took his hand.

Lazy smoke billowed from the kitchen chimney.
Theresa watched them leave and said her farewell in her heart. She

looked up at the sky, at the pristine eighteenth century world she inhabited briefly, then stretched her arms upwards to be reclaimed by a new sunset.

She sat on the attic chair and held the book close to her. Dawn broke over the harbour as Theresa held the diary, her oil of joy for mourning.

The touch of snow, the sound of kookaburras, the scent of eucalyptus, the taste of a seed, the sight of a brooch.
Theresa could sense love all around her.

Chapter 35

Anna looked across at Grace. "You must feel like total crap."

"I don't know how I feel, I'm so worried about Tess."

"How's she handling it?"

"She's crying a lot, which is good, she's getting it out of her system. Being at the hospital when Alicia went into cardiac arrest took a toll on her. But she sits in the attic and cries, not downstairs. Says it helps her." Her eyes filled. "I don't know what else to do for her."

"Just be there for her, especially when she backs away. Kids just wanna know you love them, especially when they totally reject you." Grace groped for the tissue box, knocking over her pen holder.

Anna picked up the spill and handed the tissues to her. "Boss, your daughter's right, your eyesight's appalling."

Grace laughed. "I know. That's the first time I've laughed this week." She caught sight of her reflection in the window.

"God, I look a hundred years old!" She dabbed cover stick over her nose and cheeks.

"You've looked better, boss. How's the kid doin' at hospital?"

"Surprisingly well. The drip she's on has improved her body weight and she's conscious again. They're going to check for neural damage this week but Tess says she seems fine. My girl's been to see her every afternoon after Tafe." Her eyes welled again. "She's such a sweetie." Grace groaned "I can't cry any more, I've just reapplied my makeup!"

"Your budget meeting's on with Mr Gordon in one hour. That should stem the flow."

"Just the thought of it does the trick. Thanks, Anna."

"Don't thank me, get me a raise."

"Do you know I was asked to stay on after December?"

"No surprises there, they never find a mug to stay for long. What did you say?"

"I said I'd consider it, if they offered a salary increase. Obviously, it also depends on how Tess feels about it."

"How do you feel?"

"Kinda excited. I've meet some great people at bellydancing, we're going to a Turkish restaurant tomorrow night."

"Good for you, boss, a Saturday night date. Give Tess time, kids rebound faster than we think. How'd she enjoy staying with her dad?"

"OK, I think, we've barely spoken about it. I think Stephan did his usual trick and caught up on gardening while the missus was away. She saw Nick while she was there, apparently it didn't go so well."

"Poor kid, she's had it on all fronts."

Grace's eyes threatened tears again.

"I thought we'd take a long weekend next week, stay in the Blue Mountains. Get away from everything."

"Excellent idea. Take the handsome artist with you."

"Whoa, too fast for me. We're going out to dinner though."

"Very cosy, what brought that on?"

"A glass of scotch."

Anna laughed as Grace gave a sheepish grin. "I think it'll be fun, a good starting point for me."

"Does he know you're using him as a social experiment? or is it just for sex?"

"Anna, it's not like that!"

"Sure."

"Think what you like, missy. Peter's very sweet but he'd never fit into my life. It'd be like having a tropical plant in my cold Melbourne garden. I'd have to fuss and agonize over it for it to survive. I want someone who'd fit in easily, someone I could trust."

"Now you're prejudging him, missy. I won't lecture, you're a big girl."

Anna glanced at her watch. "We need cappuccinos, boss. While I'm outside, I'll look for the perfect man for you. He'll be so uncomplicated and obvious, I'm sure I'll just trip over him."

"Make mine a weak tea, it's a bit late in the day for a caffeine hit." Grace sighed and stared out the window.

A seaplane hovered over the Harbour Bridge. Grace liked the cocky tilt of its frame, it seemed an allegory of her life now.

She turned away and scanned the documents on her desk.

Chapter 36

Theresa sat on the bus and watched people enter.

"Do you always stare at people like that?" Ruan whispered in her ear.

"Yeah, I can't help it. Ever since I was a little girl I used to watch people."

"You were some weird kid."

"Still am," she grinned. "Don't you find people fascinating? Look at the old lady up the front with her shopping trolley, bet she lives alone with five cats and the trolley's full of cat food. That girl behind her with the blue hair? Probably sings in a jazz band."

"Bizarre. I'll have to be careful introducing you to people." Ruan leaned closer. "It was good of your mum to invite me over for dinner."

"You haven't tried her cooking yet. When do you start working the night shift again?"

"Another week, Dad wanted me to take a couple of weeks off. He's a good old guy."

She squeezed his hand.

"Millers Point, that's us." They jostled their way off the bus. The Rocks district was quiet, the Friday night exodus of workers hadn't begun.

Theresa and Ruan walked past the quaint shopfronts till they reached the sign. Theresa's eyes filled and Ruan slipped an arm about her.

"I'll try your game, perve on people in the street. See that guy over there, with the tattoos and brown boots? He's an axe murderer, just released from Goulburn jail."

She smiled.

"And the girl sitting in front of the Museum of Art? Just about to steal a Whitely painting to pay for her fiances' bail. I like this game."

Theresa was laughing as they turned into Argyle street.

"Sorry it didn't work out with your guy in Melbourne."

"Yeah," she looked at her watch. "Mum probably won't be home yet, so I'll have'ta start cooking."

They walked on in the salty air till they reached the terrace.

Ruan opened the gate and let her pass through. "I thought Alicia looked good today. Wait till they let her out of hospital and we can take over."

"I don't think that's gonna happen, Ruan."

Maruska opened the front door and a child and her mother walked out.

The little girl smiled with brace filled teeth. "Bye Madame, see you next week."

"Goodbye, Nina."

Theresa and Ruan let them pass.

"So the genesis seed was a success?" Maruska raised an eyebrow.

"No, different person. Maruska, this is Ruan, a friend from Tafe."

"Come in for a cup of tea, cherubs. I haven't heard Grace arrive yet."

"Thanks."

Ruan's long frame suited the grand proportions of the hallway. He whistled as they walked into the kitchen. "Great place, I love Kookaburra stoves. You can make the best casseroles in them."

"You like to cook?"

"Love it, my dad's in the game."

"I admire chefs, the way they toss ingredients together and it tastes marvellous. I'm more a sandwich and cup of tea girl myself."

Theresa watched as they laughed easily together. She glanced at the shelf above the stove and Maruska spoke. "Do you need some more seeds? There's lots in the green jar."

"I don't. I threw them away, he didn't want one. Thanks anyway."

"Grace told me about your friend, I'm sorry you've gone through all that worry."

"She's Ruan's friend too."

Maruska poured tea as Ruan walked across to the stove. He lifted the jar down and opened the cork top. "What's the mystery here?"

Theresa put her hand out and he tipped some seeds onto her palm. "They're genesis seeds. Maruska and I knew someone who used them once."

He took one in his hands and smelt it.

"I know these, they're great for you." He swallowed it. "In Spain, we say they make you look with clear eyes at the one you love." He glanced at Theresa quickly. "Hey, it's true."

Theresa swallowed, aware of Maruska's eyes.

Maruska nodded at Ruan. "Have you ever played piano? You have a musician's hands."

"Nup, I learned classical guitar for ten years but I stopped about three years ago. It's funny, I was telling Dad last night that I wanna take it up again. I miss it, y'know, miss the motion with my fingers. It takes you away to a safe place."

"Exactly."

The front door opened and Grace rushed down the hallway. "Don't rush, my dear. They're with me."

"Good evening, Maruska. Hi you two, sorry I'm late. I'll head up and start dinner, come up when you're ready."

Grace ran up the stairs, corporate notes and shopping bags balanced in both hands. The smell of oil paints aromatic as she approached the first floor.

Peter's door was open, he stood in a corner of the room in front of a canvas. His grey hair caught the light, the square spread of his shoulders caught her heart. Brighton beach softly washed over her.

He glanced up. "Good evening, Grace. Don't forget our date."

"How could I?" She held up her shopping bags to Peter. "I'm cooking for three tonight. You're welcome to join us."

"What's on the menu?"

"Salmon and potatoes, probably overcooked and overboiled."

"Just the way I like 'em. I'll bring up a bottle."

"OK, give me half an hour." She smiled and walked upstairs.

"God help me," she thought, "I'm about to poison four people in one go." She squinted at her keys.

Theresa and Ruan followed behind and Theresa took her keys and opened the door.

Ruan lifted the shopping bags from Grace and walked to the kitchen.

"Thanks. How long have you been waiting for me, Tess?"

"Not long, Maruska invited us in for tea."

Grace stared blankly at the fridge.

"You OK, Mum?"

"I'm a crap cook. Peter'll be here in half an hour, you have to help me. If I burn everything, I can blame you."

Ruan peered inside the bags. "What's cooking?"

"Supposedly salmon, potatoes and spinach but I'm having a panic attack."

"No worries, I'll take over. Tess, can you get me a pot and a lemon squeezer. I'll peel the potatoes if you could squeeze a lemon. Where do you keep your olive oil, Grace?"

Grace kissed him. "Thank you, I can't do this tonight. I'll get changed, then I'll set the table for you. I can make a decent salad." She hurried down the hallway.

Theresa leaned on the kitchen bench and looked at Ruan. "So, what is the genesis seed?"

"A pepper seed, I've been eating them since I was in my high chair."

"Is that all it is? I thought it was something magical."

"Shows what you know about cooking." His eyes reflective. "Maybe the magic is in the giving."

"My mum thinks you're an angel."

"What do you think I am?"

She walked over to him, stood on her tiptoes and kissed him softly on the cheek.

"Mine."

He kissed her right back.

Theresa could see love as a little girl.

Postscript

Jonathon stood on the Ponte Vecchio bridge in Florence and admired the city. Sandstone buildings and elegant carriages caught his eye.
He kissed the urn in his arms and held it aloft.
"You're home."
With one hand, he opened the silver seal and tilted the urn. The ashes fell to the river Arno below.

A wind hovered on the water, then raised itself along the river banks. It caught the ashes in a whirlpool and sent them on their path. Far. Wide. High.
High as heaven they blew.